TTEO

TAKE THE EMOTION OUT

REN LAWS

Acknowledgments

My thanks to family, friends and others who have supported me on this new journey.

I journey to a destination unknown, riding a carriage of possibilities, in the pursuit of a life lived.

ಲ೦೦ಜಲ

INDEX

1. A CHANCE

The street below my bedroom window was empty. The morning sun shyly peaked out from behind clouds bathing the street in weak sunlight. It was early November. The trees still held leaves with an array of autumn colours. I sighed and looked down at the letter in my hand. Slow steps moved me to my bed. I sat down smoothing the orange duvet cover and placing a pillow encased in the same orange shade between my back and the headboard. I shifted slightly as I swung my legs up. I placed another pillow on my lap and rested my hands on it focusing on the letter. The words "offer" and "three Bs" jumped out at me.

Going through the university clearing system was not my fate after all. The letter arrived later than expected, giving me an extended stay in limbo. My other two university choices responded with prompt rejections.

I managed to grab the letter before anyone noticed it. My first university choice, the University of Birmingham, made me an offer to study Law and Business Studies. I want to stay close to home, close to Amada. I also want to save on all the costs of having to pay for accommodation. I don't fancy the idea of having a huge debt by the time I complete three years of study. Getting a degree should not necessarily mean starting out my next chapter with the burden of being in massive debt.

I brought my attention back to the letter. I now had a clear possibility, making it a reality is a hurdle I must get over. Three Bs wouldn't be easy for me to achieve, but I would have a bloody good go at it. If I worked harder than I have ever worked, maybe I could pull it off.

I closed my eyes - come on Brissy Jayne Yah, you can do this! I opened my eyes and smiled, I had a chance to go to university, I had a chance! Thank you, God, thank you! Air filled my lungs as I inhaled deeply through my nose and exhaled loudly through my mouth. My new chapter was within my grasp.

My eyes roamed the familiarity of my room – my sanctuary. This space held me securely for so many good years. The walls wore a variety of colours over the years. I painted them white about a year ago. The blank canvas held two items that provided splashes of vivid colours. My Egyptian tapestry depicting figures in elaborate and colourful ancient costumes. A painted canvas of the silhouettes of three African women wearing gowns in orange, green, and red. The tapestry and painting represent the two halves that, made me whole.

A knock on my bedroom door interrupted my thoughts, the door opened before I could respond. The tall lean frame of my foster brother stood in the doorway.

Marcus and I have been friends since David and Claire Morgan became my foster parents when I was twelve years old. Marcus and his younger sister Grace were already living with Amado and Amada (these are the affectionate Spanish titles we gave David and Claire, it meant beloved one). The fourteen-year-old Marcus and ten-year-old Grace welcomed me and shown kindness. In the nurturing care of Amado and Amada we all flourished. My remote default and disengagement from others improved. I am the first to admit that when it comes to my emotions, I remained a control freak.

"Well?" Marcus asked as he entered and closed the door behind him. I guess I was not quite as stealthy as I thought. I had been seen removing my letter from the bundle of post. My eyes travelled to his grey stare.

"Marcus Findall, when will you learn to wait to be invited in before you enter my bedroom?" I gave him a hard stare.

Marcus dropped his tall frame on the bed. Took the pillow on my lap and placed it under his elbow. He propped his head on his hand and twisted his body to face me. He eyed the letter in my hand.

"Are you going to tell me what the letter says?"

I shook my head, exasperated. "I could have been in my birthday suit, how embarrassing would that have been?"

"Well, you're not," his eyes moved briefly over my body, "only a Nun could be more decently dressed. Besides, you don't have anything that I haven't seen before." His tone was mocking.

"I don't doubt that you have seen many naked women, but you have not seen me. Not all women are equally endowed." I tried to look superior but did not quite pull it off.

Marcus chuckled, his eyes filling with amusement.

"You give yourself too much credit."

The letter was now lying on the bed between us. Marcus picked it up and read it quickly. He slowly raised his eyes to meet my gaze. A warm smile spread over his face.

"I knew you would get an offer; this is fantastic news. Congratulations, BJ!" He sat up and gave me a hug and kiss on the cheek. He placed the pillow on his back and leaned against the headboard, matching my own position.

"Thanks, getting three Bs will not be easy, hoping I can swing it."

"I have complete faith in you, you can do it. I am glad you will be staying home. I will be able to keep an eye on you."

"Do I need an eye kept on me?" I glanced at the window and watched the weak streams of sunlight.

"No, it's more for my benefit than yours. I worry about you, despite you being more sensible than my eighty-year-old gran." I could not help smiling, Marcus' gran was quite a character. I turned to face him.

"Well, if there is ever a time to kick up my heels and go mad, that time will be when I am a first-year university student. Sex, alcohol, an assortment of drugs and hunks galore, what more could a girl ask for?"

"That's not you, BJ. Don't go changing."

"No, it's not me now, but who knows. It is inevitable that I will change on some level, the degree of change remains to be seen. Let's just say I am looking forward to new experiences." Marcus gave me a measured look.

"What new experience are you looking forward to? Is it the new levels of academic stimulation, the consumption of alcohol and other substances or is it sex?"

"Don't worry Marcus. I could never match your appetite for variety. You dear Marcus, are …" I paused, "how can I put this politely?" I gave him a cheeky smile. "The only description that comes to mind is tart with a capital T!" Marcus' eyes widened and filled with laughter.

"How dear you! I see myself more as a connoisseur of all things beautiful. Beautiful women happen to be the top of the list of the many things that I have an appreciation for." I scoffed at his words.

"Which little beauty are you currently appreciating?"

"A secondee at work, nice girl. Our relationship is as simple as it gets."

"Like I said – a tart!" Marcus took the pillow from behind him and whacked me with it. I picked up my pillow and hit him over the head with it. We looked at each other laughing and yelled at the same time.

"Pillow fight!" Neither of us had mercy on the other as we bashed each other with pillows. Hysterical laughter filled my room.

"What is all this commotion?" My foster mother – Amada entered my room. She rolled her eyes at the sight of us. Her voice distracted Marcus for a second. I delivered a lethal blow with my pillow. He lost his balance and toppled off my bed. I jumped off my bed and raised my arms in the air. In a mock sports commentator voice, I said.

"Winner! Brissy Jayne Yah delivers a knockout blow and wins the pillow fight." Marcus lay in an undignified heap on the floor howling with laughter. Amada shook her head.

"You two should remember that you are not children anymore." We regained our composure and kept a straight face with some difficulty.

"We should all go out for dinner tonight. BJ has some great news we should celebrate." Marcus waved his hand in a gesture inviting me to share my news. I looked at Amada with a big smile on my face.

"I have an offer from the University of Birmingham, I need to get three Bs." Amada shrieked and rushed over to me wrapping me in a hug.

"Oh, honey, that is wonderful news. I knew you would get an offer. Marcus is right we should celebrate. Let's have dinner at Chick Chick. I know you never get tired of their spicy chicken. Grace will be thrilled at your news too. I will leave you to tell her when she wakes up."

"That sounds great, Amada. Can we postpone the celebrations until next weekend? I have already made plans to meet Funmi and her cousin Emmanuel for lunch, and I am going to try and catch-up with Nikki afterwards. I have not seen or heard from her in a while."

"Sure, honey. I will book a table for the four of us next week Sunday. I have some errands to run in town, then I am popping over to visit Edna. I will be home before 5:00 PM." Marcus checked his watch.

"Can I get a lift with you to the garage? The MOT and servicing on my car is done. I said I would pick it up by 11:15 AM." Amada nodded.

"See you later, alligator," said Marcus. I gave him a salute in return.

"See you later, honey, you should wear something special for dinner next weekend." There was a mischievous twinkle in Amada's eye as she followed Marcus out of my room. I wonder what she is up to.

Some fresh air and time to think would be good before I headed out for my lunch date with Funmi and Emmanuel. I paused to examine my image in the full-length mirror on my wardrobe door. My oval face was surrounded by shoulder length brown hair, a mass of kinky curls, with streaks of lighter shades of brown. My full lips were lightly smeared with a natural shade lip gloss, I wrinkled my small snub nose. My almond shaped eyes are my most striking feature, they are amber. Wolf eyes, that's what my mother used to say.

My chocolate-coloured skin was clear and make-up free. People often assessed my looks with interest, intrigued by my ethnic heritage.

My mother and her side of the family came from Egypt. My father was Nigerian. He died of cancer before I was born. From the few pictures I had seen of him, he was a tall dark-skinned man with a solid frame. Even in pictures his face conveyed warmth, humour, and kindness. My height and colouring were the only obvious things I took from him. I stood at 5 feet 11 inches. My body was not built to be thin. I examined my full breasts, curvy hips, and generous bottom.

I struggled with my body image during my early teens. Thankfully, I can now say that I am comfortable with my form. I was dressed casually in snug fitting jeans and a grey and white mock shirt jumper.

I grabbed my bag and left my room. Grace would not appear until around midday. Anyone who tried to wake her before she was ready on a weekend was taking their life in their hands. I slowly made my way towards the stairs looking at the array of family photos on the walls. They always gave me a warm and secure feeling. I felt incredibly grateful. Being placed with Amada and Amado had been a wonderful gift.

From the age of twelve years, I grew up in a loving, supportive, and close-knit family. Prior to that, I spent three disorientated and unhappy years with two other families. I stopped in front of a family photo that included my foster father, Amado. He died in a terrible car accident when I was fifteen years old. It had been an incredibly sad time for us all. He was still dearly missed. I reached out and touched Amado's image and said a quiet prayer for him, then went down the stairs.

I put on my coat, picked up my house keys and left. I headed for Cannon Hill Park; it was a short walk from home. I drew my hood over my head and pulled on my gloves. It was cold but not freezing. The sun shirked its shyness and was now shining brightly. The seasonal changes struck me. Five years or so ago, a November day such as today would be freezing cold. Global warming was real, I did not understand why some still denied it was a serious problem. My mother loved the winter months. Long walks on a cold winter day had been her speciality.

We live in Edgbaston, in the south part of the city. It is not the millionaire part, but it is a nice part of Birmingham. None of us are originally from Birmingham. I lived in London until I was eleven years old when I moved to Birmingham with my mother after my gran died. Amada and Amado moved to Birmingham from London over fifteen years ago. Marcus and Grace lived in Milton Keynes before they came to live with an aunt in Birmingham. I like Birmingham and its surrounding areas. The city had a welcoming feeling. I felt at home here and didn't plan to move back to London.

Cannon Hill Park is one of my favourite places in the city. Its vast 250 acres had something to offer everyone. I also loved the Midlands Art Centre, the MAC. It is located at the Edgbaston Road entrance to the park. I left Edgbaston Road, walked past the MAC, and entered the park. My eyes were treated to an assortment of autumn colours. Heading away from the boating lake, I made my way towards the centre of the park. After about 5 minutes' walk, I came to a quiet spot, and sat on a bench. I took my offer letter out of my bag. I looked down at the letter and read it slowly. I have to confirm my acceptance of the offer by email, the response deadline is in seven days.

I leaned back on the bench, feeling a renewed sense of purpose. I can do this. It had been a long and rocky road that led me to this point. I was bright but my ability to excel was hindered by a learning difference. It was a challenge that could, perhaps, be better managed if I sought help. I recognised that my approach may not be the best. I was not willing to risk anyone telling me my own limitations.

I knew that this would not necessarily be the case. But still I shied away from specific support. Believing, that if I work hard enough, I will get there. I had become well practised at finding ways to compensate for my weaknesses. Sometimes at considerable cost, but I figured there is a price to pay for most things in life. I am not unique.

Rightly or wrongly, like most issues or challenges in my life, I preferred to manage them myself rather than involve others. It was something I was still working on doing better at. Reliance on others was, in my mind, an exposure. A risk that was best avoided.

I managed my learning difference by working harder than most of my peers. I pay attention to myself when it comes to what works for me. It typically takes me longer to do certain activities. But once completed, the standards I achieved were usually better than average. My learning difference was something I once saw as a defect. Now I see it as a double-edged sword. One side of the sword was sharp. When it cuts, as it frequently did, it hurts like hell. The other side of the sword gifted me with creativity, resilience, and perseverance. Many of the things about my character that I value.

"May I sit?" My head jerked up to meet the brown eyes of an elderly man.

"Yes." I gave him a small smile. He sat down and rested his hands on the silver knob of his cane; a lion's head was carved into it.

"It is a beautiful day. The sort of day that makes you thankful to be alive." He gazed ahead as he spoke. What accent is that? His voice was cultured, with pleasant mellow tones. He had a shock of white wavy hair on his head and a neat white beard. The olive tone skin on his face and hands were creased with fine lines. He was well dressed, his wool coat looked expensive.

"Yes, I love autumn." He nodded his agreement. Something was amusing him, the corners of his lips curved in a brief smile. I followed his gaze. He was watching two little boys playing out a Jedi fight scene with their lightsabers. The fight intensified, one of the boys tripped and fell on the grass, the other boy raised his lightsaber high above his head as if to deliver a fatal blow. The boy on the ground kicked him on the ankle. He howled in pain, lost his balance, and fell. The boy who fell first scrabbled up pointing his weapon at his victim who was still wailing in pain. The elderly man chuckled.

"It is part of the human make up to want to win. To want to be the first amongst many. We have so much potential. Our mind is an untapped powerhouse, capable of so much more than we can imagine. We focus our efforts on exploring other planets when the most reachable unexplored frontier is the human brain." He turned to look at me, studying my face. An unfathomable emotion briefly flickered in his eyes. He nodded and got up.

"Thank you, my dear, for listening to an old man's wandering mind. Take care of yourself." He turned and walked away before I could respond. I watched him until he was out of sight.

My brows knitted together. The old man was right about one thing. The mind is indeed unchartered territory. Most people did not have a clue about what their mind was capable of. I wish I could count myself amongst the clueless.

Last night, I had the dream again. A man with golden eyes was chasing me through a forest. Though his eyes were visible in the dark, like on the other occasions, I couldn't see his face clearly. I fell and rolled down a bank and landed near the shore of a lake. A golden light was coming from the lake. I walked to the edge of the water bending to look at the light. My hand reached out and touched the water. The earth shook and a loud rumbling sound came from the lake. My fear was palpable as I moved away from the water's edge.

A wave suddenly rose, poured three pools of water around me then retreated to the lake. The three pools rose into human forms with golden eyes. They pointed to me and said the familiar words – *'The time for the awakening is upon you, Brissy Jayne Yah. Soon you will be awake.'* As always, I woke up after the words were spoken.

Variations of the dream had plagued me for the last six months. Two things remained consistent, a man with the golden eyes chasing me, and the words that were spoken.

The dreams rattled me because I knew a version of it was likely to become reality. Since I turned thirteen, my dreams were more like premonitions. I had never shared this weird fact with anyone. I considered telling Marcus, but I always wavered at the last minute. There seemed to be a link between my migraines and the dreams. Another one of my odd bod markers. I was notching up quite a few of them.

I sighed deeply and shifted with discomfort on the bench. My discomfort had little to do with the hard bench. My mind strayed to a conversation with Amada six months earlier. She pressed harder for me to agree to see a counsellor. She had been trying to get me to do this for a while. I knew she was anxious about when I go to university. She wanted me to try and work on some of my emotional issues before I left home. I knew that staying home whilst I attend university would make her happy.

I love Amada dearly. I didn't want her to worry about me, so I promised to attend at least 6 counselling sessions after my exams. It had not been too difficult to convince her to wait for me to complete the final year of my A Levels. I knew that now was not the time to start delving into dark and unpredictable places in my mind. I needed to hang on tightly to the knowns in my life. I need to have a clear head to get through my exams. All I want is the status quo, a free mind, and no additional complications.

I was startled back to the present by the laughter and jovial screams of a group of young teenagers heading in my direction. I got up and walked towards the Edgbaston Road exit. I headed for the bus stop on the Pershore Road. I could catch a bus to Birmingham city centre from there. It was a short journey. I had three bus options; it did not take long before I got on a bus. The bus was not too busy. I sat on one of the raised seats towards the back of the bus, pushed off my hood and placed my bag on the seat next to me.

Pershore Road is a long arterial road that runs through south Birmingham. I looked out of the window. The bus approached Calthorpe Park which is on the opposite side of the road. Joggers, dog walkers, and families were enjoying the good weather. One of the things I love about Birmingham is how green it is. Open green spaces are in abundant supply in the city.

ഇ౦ൻ౦

2. FAVOURITE PEOPLE

The bus approached my stop. I got up, rang the bell, and made my way to the door. Moments later I was making my way through the shoppers. The Bistro was just a five minutes' walk from the bus stop. I made my way through the hustle and bustle of the city centre, dodging shoppers with multiple bags. The Bistro was in sight, Funmi and Emmanuel appeared from the street corner ahead of me. They saw me straight away and waved. A big smile spread across my face. I waved back. Funmi jogged towards me with her arms held out wide.

"Brissy!" Yelled Funmi. I broke into a run and held my arms outwards. We both uttered little screams as we met in an embrace. It was wonderful to see my fun-loving friend. Since leaving school, we don't see nearly enough of each other.

"Brissy, I haven't seen you in over two months. I have missed you. Let's take a look at you." Funmi held me at arm's length and cast her sharp eyes over my face and form. "You look beautiful as always - Miss au naturelle. I don't know anyone who looks as good as you with virtually no make-up." She hugged me again, I wound my arms around her waist, and we rocked back and forth.

"It is so good to see you, Funmi. I have missed you too!"

"Hey, Brissy. Nice to see you again." Emmanuel's cockney twang made us both look in his direction. He hung back and was observing the commotion that Funmi and I were causing with amusement.

"Hello Emmanuel, great to see you. This is your second visit to Birmingham in three months, are you getting bored of London?" I gave Emmanuel a teasing smile. He made a melodramatic gesture putting one hand out with his palm facing upwards and resting his other hand on his heart, a look of mock horror on his face.

"Get tired of London, never!" He said in his usual dramatic style. Funmi and I burst out laughing. "Birmingham does have its attractions." He moved forward and gave me a kiss on the cheek. I laughed at his blatant flirtatious tone. My phone rang. I released Funmi to fish it out of my bag.

"Khadijah, hi!" I am pleased to hear from her. I sent the lunch invitation out last night but had not received a response from her and Nikki. I had been friends with the two of them and Funmi since secondary school.

"Hi Brissy, I just realised that I didn't respond to your message. Me and Nikki just finished our shift. Is lunch still on?" Khadijah and Nikki had been working at a department store in the city centre every Saturday since they were sixteen.

"Absolutely, just met up with Funmi and Emmanuel, we're about to go into The Bistro."

"OK, see you in ten minutes".

"Great." I did a little dance.

"Khadijah and Nikki will be joining us in about ten minutes. It must be my lucky day. I am going to be in the company of so many of my favourite people!" I laughed.

"Fabulous, let's go grab a table. It's going to be a good afternoon," said Funmi. She raised her arms in the air and gave a 'Woohoo', Emmanuel smiled, shaking his head. We entered The Bistro full of energy and laughter. The restaurant was busy, but a good selection of empty tables could be seen from where we stood. A waitress approached us with a smile.

"Hello, is it just the three of you?" she asked, reaching for menus.

"We need a table for five, please," I responded.

"This way, please." The waitress led us to a table towards the rear of the restaurant. We had a good view of the entrance to the restaurant. It was perfect. The waitress placed the menus next to each place setting.

"Shall I return in five minutes to take your order?"

"Yes please," said Funmi, as we sat down. I sat between Funmi and Emmanuel. We hung our coats at the back of our chairs. Emmanuel poured us each a glass of water from the jug on the table.

"That's a lovely dress, Funmi. Is it part of your new collection?" Funmi is an A Level fashion student. She is incredibly talented. She made three of my favourite outfits in my wardrobe. The dress she was wearing was striking. The front and back of her dress were made of a copper knit material, the high neck and long sleeves were made from black mesh lace. The dress clung to Funmi's slim body, it reached just above her knees. She wore black ribbed tights; and brown leather two-inch heeled ankle boots completed the stylish outfit. Funmi's make up was done perfectly. Her close crop natural afro hair was dyed blond. She presented a striking image. As always, she held herself with complete confidence and ease.

"Thanks sweetie. It's an experiment for a new theme I am working on for my end of year fashion show. It's centred around the use of bold colours and contrasts in materials. I am really pleased with how this dress turned out. By the way, I am still waiting for your confirmation that you will loan me that fabulous figure of yours, to model a couple of outfits. I have some ambitious plans in mind for the fashion show. Pretty please." She batted her eye lashes at me.

"How could I possibly resist such charm. I would be honoured to be your mannequin."

"Thanks! I'm going to have so much fun creating two of the outfits for you. I have some great ideas already. One of your outfits will be the centre piece of my collection. A dress integrating traditional African fabrics and colours. I am going to dress you like a sexy African queen." She rubbed her hands together in glee.

"I can't wait to see what Funmi cooks up for you, I am definitely attending the fashion show." Emmanuel gave a little wolf whistle. Funmi winked at him.

"You are in for a treat. Brissy will be wearing the waist beads I asked your mum to pick up on her next trip to Nigeria." My eyes widened.

"Funmi, please tell me that all my essential bits will remain covered." She gave me a cheeky smile.

"Of course, I promise you will love it. You'll need to get your hair braided to complete the look. I am so excited about the dress. It's going to be what I want my name to inspire as a designer. You know how I dream of promoting the use of African fabrics, prints and accessories. The dress is going to be my first major piece that will embody that dream." I smiled at the look on her face and the passion in her voice. "Oh, I forgot to tell you Brissy – Kade is home. For good this time. He's got a flat on Edward Road in Edgbaston. It'll be great to have him close by. He asked after you." Funmi looked at me and waggled her eyebrows. Kade is Funmi's older brother from her mum's first marriage. He'd been in the Army. I ignored the expression on her face and responded.

"That's nice, how does he feel about leaving the Army? I guess it will take a little getting used to after five years of service." Kade joined the Army when he was sixteen years old.

"He decided about a year ago that five years was his cut off point. I think he is now looking forward to making a new life for himself. We are all relieved to have him home safe."

I glanced at the restaurant doors and saw Khadijah and Nikki enter. Relieved to be given an opportunity to steer the conversation away from Kade. I stood up and waved at them, my face beaming. They waved back and made their way to our table; I left my seat to greet them.

"Long time no see, it's wonderful to see you both." Khadijah reached me first. I gave her a big hug and a kiss on the cheek then turned to Nikki. I threw my arms around her petite body. "Hello, my angel, how are you?" Nikki hugged me back. I had not seen her in six weeks. I held her at arm's length and inspected her face. My eyebrows knitted together. There was a fading bruise on Nikki's cheek and a sad look in her eyes. I hugged her again and whispered in her ear. "We need to talk." She gave me a little smile and a brief nod.

Nikki has been avoiding my calls for several weeks. The last time we spoke, we had a difficult conversation about her boyfriend, and his crappy behaviour. Nikki was no push over by any measure, but she has a big heart. Tending to want to give people a second and sometimes third chance. But, when she put her foot down, little could change her mind. We joined the others at the table and took our seats.

"It is so great to socialise again. I haven't been out in almost two months. Promised my parents that I would cut back on socialising. They are worried about how much work I have to get through for my exams." Khadijah rolled her large brown eyes as she ended her comments. She was a natural high achiever. She intended to go to university to study biotechnology. I didn't doubt that she would put in the work required and get the grades she needed. She gathered her long dark hair off her shoulders with her hands and let it fall down her back.

"A new guy joined our department a couple of weeks ago. Gorgeous George is a quiet one. I think he quite fancies Nikki, I caught him checking out her ass today."

"Khadijah!" Nikki's face turned red as she gave Khadijah an indignant look.

"Come on Nikki, you have to admit he is a looker."

"Yes, he is good looking, but I am not interested." Nikki's tone was stilted.

"What about you, Emmanuel, what's new?" I asked. He gave me a speculative look but decided to play along. Emmanuel is 19 years old and already attending university studying Architecture.

"I am off to Shanghai in a couple of weeks. It's a two weeks' trip organised by my uni to take in interesting buildings, including Sky Soho built by Dame Zaha Mohammad Hadid. The building looks fantastic in pictures, full of sexy curves and lines. Women architects are great at injecting curves into buildings. No one does it better than Dame Zaha Mohammad Hadid – the queen of the curve!"

"I read an article about her. It said she was the first woman to receive some top architecture award."

"Yes, the Pritzker Architecture Prize. It's my dream to win it one day."

"She sounds like a real trail blazer. Always great to hear about women who have shown men how things are done!" Khadijah said.

"Don't forget us when you hit the big time." I said teasingly to Emmanuel. He leaned towards me, holding my gaze.

"You, Brissy, are quite unforgettable." He gave me a slow smile. I cleared my throat.

"How is that rascal little brother of yours?"

Emmanuel laughed softly. "Dipo is good, thanks. Up to no good as usual. Last week he announced to us all during dinner that he was in love. Mum said an eight-year-old should have other things on his mind. He turned to her and asked her what impresses girls, and how do you get them to like you." We all burst out laughing.

"My little cousin is ahead of the game!" Funmi gave us a proud wink.

"So, ladies, would you care to answer my little brother's question? What do you want from your man, Brissy, and what would impress you?"

"Do you really want to know?" He nodded enthusiastically.

"There's a song I love that sums it up nicely." I belted out the first few lines from the chorus of Bruno Mars' *Just the Way You are*. "Back me up girls." The girls joined in and we sang the rest of the chorus. Emmanuel clapped in delight.

"Bravo ladies!" I glanced around the restaurant. There were many eyes on our table.

The light-hearted banter continued. We dived right in with updates on what we had all been up to over the last couple of months or so. Funmi, Khadijah and Emmanuel provided many side-splitting snapshots of their recent escapades and encounters. By the time I looked at my phone it was 3:00 PM. I had laughed so hard I was dabbing away tears. The repeated loud episodes of hysteria were not appreciated by all our fellow diners. Khadijah sighed.

"My next study and revision session will start in an hour; I have to get going. Sticking to my schedule is my new religion." Why don't we try and meet up once every month for lunch? It will be some much-needed relief. We're all going to be working bloody hard over the next five to six months. What do you think?"

There was unanimous agreement around the table, with a caveat from Emmanuel that he would attend if in Birmingham when we meet.

"I have to go too. I promised my mum I would be home before 4:00 PM to look after my sister," said Nikki.

"I will walk you home and take a cab home from your place," I said. I want the chance to speak to her. She was not slipping off and avoiding me again.

"Sounds good," responded Nikki without meeting my gaze. We settled the bill and said our goodbyes.

ಐ ಲ ಐ

3. UNACCEPTABLE

Nikki lives in Hockley about a mile and a half from the city centre. The walk would give us plenty of time to talk. I hooked my arm through hers as we walked towards the Jewellery Quarter area of the city.

"How have you been, Nikki?" I cast a sideways glance at her.

"Not bad, thanks. You?" Her response was light. She started biting the corner of her lip. I recognised her tell.

"I'm OK. Relieved and pleased about my offer." I shared my good news with everyone over lunch. Nikki turned to give me a beaming smile.

"I am happy for you, and so glad that you will be staying in Birmingham. I have been worrying about what I am going to do without my best friend nearby." When we left secondary school, Nikki was undecided as to what she wanted to do. She decided that vocational training would suit her better than going to university. She got a job as a receptionist at a local dentist. About eight months ago she decided that she wanted to train to be a dental nurse. Her apprenticeship at Birmingham Dental Hospital starts next September.

"Thanks. Why have you been avoiding me?"

"Life has just been hectic. I'm sorry I've not been in touch."

"Life has been a little more than hectic, Nikki. I think you've been avoiding me, and I think it's got something to do with Carl. You can either talk now as we walk or I can camp out at your house, and badger you till you tell me the truth. What's it to be?" She stopped and looked at me. I held her stare.

"You've got that look on your face. Fine, let's talk as we walk. Marsha will be all over you when we get in. We won't get any peace." Marsha is Nikki's six-year-old sister.

"OK. How did you get that bruise on your cheek?"

Nikki pulled at my arm and we continued walking. "Carl hit me three days ago. I didn't even see it coming. We went out for dinner, one of the waiters was particularly friendly. Carl mentioned that he thought the waiter fancied me. I made a joking comment about the waiter being easy on the eye. The evening went well, nothing out of the ordinary. When we got back to his flat, I went into the kitchen to make coffee. He came up behind me," her voice cracked. She cleared her throat and continued. "He started to touch me roughly. I pushed him away and asked what the hell was wrong with him. That's when he hit me and called me a slut. He accused me of wanting to sleep with the waiter.

He ranted on like a crazy person. I was shocked and scared. I wanted to run out right then, but something told me that was a bad idea. I stayed and tried to calm him down. I suggested he go and watch the football match he recorded. Once he was settled in front of the TV, I said I was going to the bathroom. He was not paying any attention to me, so I snuck out and just ran. I got a cab home. Thankfully mum and Marsha were visiting my aunt. I had time to calm down before they got home. I made up a story about walking into the door."

She quickly wiped a tear away, straightened her shoulders and took a deep breath. I stopped walking and gave her a hug.

"I am OK. I don't want to turn into a blubbering mess." She hooked her arm through mine, we continued walking.

"I am sorry that abusive bastard did that to you. Please tell me that it's over. You are not going to see him again, are you?"

"No! I gave him a second chance after the verbal abuse. There is no way in hell I am going back to him after he hit me. I am done with him. He's been calling me; I haven't answered his calls."

"You should report him to the police."

"I just want to draw a line under the nightmare and move on. I never want to see him again. When I get home, I'll send him a message letting him know that."

"Good! He needs to be clear that he should stay the hell away from you. You need something to cheer you up, how about some retail therapy? A day of shopping followed by a movie and dinner. Dinner will be my treat.

Nikki smiled. "That sounds lovely, thanks. Enough about me, tell me about you. I hear Kade is back for good. What do you think of that?" There was a twinkle in her eye.

"I am sure it's wonderful for his family that he's home safe. Why should I think anything of it in particular?" My voice was even, and I kept my expression neutral.

"Come on, Brissy, you can't fool me! Ever since you saw him stark naked when you were fifteen, you've been carrying a torch for the guy."

"Fine. Kade, is an attractive man. Judging from the girl that was hanging on his arm at Funmi's sixteenth birthday party, his taste is more model chic. I don't think I'm his type."

"I wouldn't be so sure about that. I saw him looking at you on more than one occasion that night. There's definitely something there."

"I'm surprised you remember anything about that night other than Marcus. You two would make a great couple you know. My only concern is that Marcus is more focused on having fun than getting into anything serious."

"Ahh, the gorgeous Marcus. He is great of course, and I love that wicked sense of humour of his. But I am taking a break from men, I just want to focus on me."

"Sounds like a good idea." We were almost at Nikki's front door when a male voice called her name. We turned around to find Carl getting out of his car. He walked towards us. Nikki froze, her eyes huge in her face. I stepped between her and Carl as he stopped a few yards from us.

"You are not welcome here, Carl. What do you want?" Anger coursed through my body; how dare he show his face after what he did.

"Mind your own damn business, Brissy. Nikki can speak for herself. Come on Nikki, I made a mistake, it won't happen again, I promise. I brought a peace offering." He held out a little bag with a well-known perfume shop's branding on it. Nikki stepped forward and stood beside me.

"I don't want anything from, you Carl. We are over, do you hear me? I never want to see you again. If you come anywhere near me or my house again, I'll call the police. Get out of here!" Nikki's voice was strong and sure. She meant every word. I was proud of her resilience. Carl's smile turned into a sneer.

"You little bitch! I'll tell you when we are done, and we are not done! I have a little something that will change your mind." He took out his phone and waved it, his face full of malice.

"The last time we had sex, took a video of you naked when you were asleep. You look great on camera. That sexy body of yours will become a trending hit for sure should the video go on social media. It would be so easy to accidentally upload it for the world to view. Every man under the age of seventy would be given a real treat!" His hideously cruel laugh echoed around us.

Nikki and I stared at him in disbelief. The blood drained from her face. What a bastard! The anger I felt turned to rage. Carl needed to feel real pain, pain like he had never felt before. I wished that phone would explode and everything on it would be gone.

Carl started to shake like he was having a fit. He dropped his phone and the bag with the perfume and clapped his hands to his ears screaming. Blood dripped from his nose. The phone he dropped looked undamaged, but it then made a cracking sound. I watched in fascination as cracks appeared on the screen. I instinctively pulled Nikki back putting my arm around her waist to turn our backs to the phone. A second later there was a loud bang.

"What's happening?" Whispered Nikki, a terrified look on her face. We turned back to face Carl. He was on his knees rocking back and forth, his nose gushing with blood. His phone was in scattered pieces on the pavement. He passed out and collapsed into a heap on the floor. Nikki rushed to his side, she checked his pulse, relief spread across her face. I looked at what was left of his phone with morbid fascination.

"Brissy, he needs help." My senses snapped back into focus.

"I'll call an ambulance." I quickly dialled the emergency number and asked for an ambulance. I described Carl's condition, I was told not to move him, that an ambulance would be with us within seven minutes. Nikki was still kneeling by Carl looking down at him not knowing what to do.

"Nikki, don't move him, go and get a blanket to put over him, while we wait for the ambulance." She rushed into her house returning seconds later with a thick blanket. We spread the blanket over Carl and waited for the ambulance.

I checked the time on my phone – it was 3:30 PM. We stood in silence for a few minutes looking down at Carl.

"Brissy, what just happened? I don't understand any of it!" We heard the approaching sound of the ambulance sirens. I went to stand by the road and waved to let them know our location. The ambulance pulled to a stop next to me. The paramedics jumped out and rushed over to Carl's motionless body on the ground.

"What happened?" One of the paramedics directed the question at me.

"I don't know, he had some sort of fit." The other paramedic on the ground next to Carl frowned.

"There are bits of shattered glass embedded in his face and hands." He cast us a questioning look. He looked around and saw what was left of Carl's phone. "How did the phone get so damaged?"

"It exploded; we don't know why. We just heard a loud bang. Will he be, OK?" I asked, as he checked Carl's pulse. The other paramedic opened the back doors and pulled out the gurney.

"His pulse is strong, that's a good sign. Did he regain consciousness at any time?"

"No," replied Nikki. We watched as the paramedics lifted Carl onto the gurney and secured the straps around him.

"What hospital are you taking him to?" Nikki asked.

"The QE, will you be attending the hospital, how do you know him?"

"He is my ex-boyfriend. No, I am not coming to the hospital. I'll call his mum and let her know what's happened."

"Please write his mum's number down for me."

Nikki searched her phone found the number and called it out, I jotted it down in my pocket diary and tore out the page. Carl was being wheeled to the ambulance. He was placed in the back of the ambulance and one of the paramedics got in with him. The other paramedic closed the door. I walked over and handed him my diary page with Carl's mum's number on it.

The ambulance drove off, sirens blaring.

"Nikki, Brissy, are you both ok, what's going on?" Nikki's mum ran over to us with Marsha in tow. She just arrived home.

Nikki turned to her mum, tears flowing down her face.

"Oh mum, it's Carl. He had some sort of fit and collapsed. The ambulance is taking him to the hospital." Her mum pulled her into a hug, Nikki sobbed uncontrollably.

ജ∞ങ

4. CEREBRAL CONNECTION

I closed the front door behind me with trembling hands. I ran straight up to my room and shut the door.

What happened to Carl? I paced my room. The trembling in my hands was spreading. What happened to Carl? The question echoed in my head. My whole body started to shake violently. Sweat broke out on my forehead and ran down the back of my neck. A whimper escaped my lips. My eyes were so wide they hurt. I heard a rattling, my eyes darted to my desk. The Nefertiti penholder was rocking. I clamped my hands over my mouth as it rose clear of my desk. It suddenly shot across the room. I dropped to the floor as it whizzed past me and smashed against the wall by the door. The noise of the ceramic hitting the wall sounded so loud I screamed.

"BJ! Are you OK?" I heard Marcus shout from his room. Seconds later my bedroom door crashed open. He took in the scene before him, quick strides placed him by my side. He kneeled surveying my face. "What's wrong, are you hurt?" My voice was lost to me. "BJ, what happened?" He took my hands and pulled me up as he rose and sat me down at the foot of my bed. He sat next to me; I met his eyes.

"I am OK, sorry if I scared you." My voice quivered a little.

"What happened?" Marcus pointed to the fragments of my penholder.

"I'm not sure."

"You are shivering, maybe you are coming down with something." He placed the palm of his hand on my forehead. "It feels like you have a temperature."

"I guess I may have caught a cold… or something."

"Get into bed. I'll clean up the mess, then we can talk." Marcus made short work of cleaning my smashed penholder. "I'll give you a few minutes to get changed and into bed. Honey and lemon will help, back shortly."

"Thanks." He left and shut the door behind him.

I took off my clothes and shoved them in the laundry basket. Pulled on leggings and a T-shirt. Got into bed and sat up placing a pillow behind me. Marcus knocked on the door briefly and entered. He placed two mugs next to my alarm clock and sat on my bed.

"Honey and lemon for you, peppermint tea for me. So – what's going on?" I took a sip of my honey and lemon and placed the mug back down. My fingers picked at the edge of my duvet, my eyes staring down. Marcus placed a forefinger under my chin and lifted my head. I met his stormy sky-coloured eyes. "Tell me what happened." I took a deep breath and nodded.

"Something happened this afternoon that upset me. I was in a bit of a state when I got home." I paused; it was going to sound crazy of course. But I should say it out loud, to check my own sanity if nothing else. "I could not stop shaking, then I heard this rattling noise from my desk. My penholder was swaying, then it rose from my desk, flew across the room and hit the wall." There, it was out! My eyes were fixed on Marcus, we sat in silence for a good minute just looking at each other. I didn't have a clue what was going through his mind, though I could guess. I cleared my throat.

"For goodness' sake say something!" In typical Marcus style, he stroked his chin refusing to be rushed.

"You were rather fond of that penholder. I remember when you got it. We took a family trip to the British Museum in London. We all got to pick something from the gift shop. You immediately went for the Nefertiti head penholder. I would be surprised if you smashed it deliberately."

"I didn't touch my penholder..." I uttered each word slowly. Marcus' lips twitched slightly.

"What happened this afternoon that upset you so much?" I knew he would ask at some point, but I was still caught off guard. I hadn't decided whether to tell him. My turn to be silent. "Well? You had lunch with your mates, what went wrong?"

"Nothing, lunch was great. It was after lunch that … something happened."

"Are you going to tell me what the something is that upset you?"

"No. Let's focus on what happened here." One step at a time. I want to hear Marcus' theory on what happened to my penholder before blowing his mind further.

"You first. Tell me what you think caused your penholder to smash."

"As I said, I didn't touch my penholder. I wouldn't smash it. It means a lot to me. I was in the same spot that you found me when you came in. It scared the crap out of me when it smashed."

"Well, unless we have a ghost, whatever happened was linked to you. Though, it's said that a person as well as a place can be haunted."

"Do you think I am haunted, is that your theory?" That may explain it and what happened to Carl. "Maybe I am haunted." A smile spread across my face.

"Now you really have my attention. You prefer the idea of being haunted to whatever else you think may be going on, because that something else scares you more. I know how creepy you find all things ghostly. You are worrying me. What is your worst fear about what is going on?" I ran my hands over my face and through my hair.

"This is going to sound really weird."

"Try me."

"Strange things have recently happened when I get really upset or angry. I think my emotional state had something to do with my penholder flying across the room and smashing."

Marcus looked bewildered. "You think you somehow moved the penholder without touching it? You think you're telekinetic?" I shrugged.

"Am I crazy?"

"No, you're not crazy. Your cold is clearly messing with your head. There's got to be a more plausible explanation for what happened to your penholder than telekinesis. We can pick up this conversation later. Finish your lemon and honey and get some rest." Marcus got up taking his mug with him. He paused at the door and looked back at me. "By the way, I don't think there is anything ghostly going on either. You can take a nap without fearing ghosts." He uttered the words in a bland tone and left. I picked up my mug and sipped my drink.

My mind returned to Nikki. While Nikki's mum consoled her, I'd gathered up the pieces of Carl's phone and placed it in the perfume bag, which still had the perfume in it intact. The phone was destroyed, the Sim Card even melted at the edges, its usual pentagon shape no longer recognisable. I left the bag and its contents on the hallway table.

Nikki was in bad shape. I stayed until she was calm. She kept asking me what I thought happened. I said I didn't know. Nikki was still in shock, but she was OK. As for Carl, whilst I hoped he recovered, I can't say I am particularly sad about what happened to him. I hoped that the video of Nikki only existed on his phone, that it was gone forever. I looked myself in the eye in my wardrobe mirror and asked myself again, what happened to Carl?

Fact - I had wanted Carl to feel pain like he had never felt before. I wished for his phone to be destroyed. Each of those two things happened no sooner had the thought entered my head. The question was, did I cause those things to happen or was it some weird coincidence? Let's face it the chances of it being a coincidence were close to zero. Carl was a healthy young man. As far as I knew he had no underlying health condition that would have caused him to have a fit like that. He also held his ears like the pain was in his head, screaming "make it stop".

If I'd caused Carl to have a fit and the phone to explode, how had I done that? I couldn't remember anything like that happening before. I assessed the things I knew about myself that were outside the remit of normality. The first thing was my premonition dreams, and the second my emotional dimmer switch. None of those things would cause direct harm to another person. The evidence suggested that I'd caused Carl harm simply by thinking it.

Carl is a pig. Hitting Nikki was bad enough, but he sunk lower still. He was a despicable human being. I felt my anger rising again. I took three deep breaths willing myself to calm down. I didn't normally get angry quickly, which was good, bearing in mind that, I am probably responsible for what happened to Carl.

Although I wished Carl pain, I want to believe that if I had known that my thoughts would turn to reality, I would not have done that to him. I had to exercise more control over my emotions. Controlling my emotions was not something that I usually struggled with, quite the opposite. I now had cause to take more care.

I checked the time on my alarm clock — 5:45 PM. I could feel the familiar tightness in my temples, the first signs that I was about to have a migraine. I needed to relax, otherwise a migraine would be the consequence of continuing to give myself the Spanish Inquisition. For the rest of the evening, I would shelve the whole thing. Maybe I would get a fresh perspective tomorrow.

I closed my eyes and visualised a block of ice. The ice was hovering above flames. Slow drops of water dripped from the ice onto the flame as the ice melted. The slow drip of the melting ice increased in pace until suddenly the ice disappeared and a shower of water doused the flames until they died. My eyes flickered open. Right now, this oddity served me well.

I couldn't indulge in a normal reaction. I needed to maintain control of my emotions, more so now than ever. I could already feel the familiar distancing of myself from what happened. A nap may help my orientation. I closed my eyes and tried to relax.

I stretched under my duvet as I woke from my nap. Thankfully, I slept for a couple of hours or so, no dreams. All I needed now was something to focus on that required some mental stretch. A shower followed by a review of my study and revision schedule, would be a good use of my time. I need to get my head down and get serious with preparing for my exams. I had a plan, now I needed to execute it. I got up, stripped off my clothes, put on my robe and went to take a shower.

I relaxed as the warm jets of water hit my skin. Lingering in the shower a little longer than usual. When I stepped out, the tenseness in my muscles felt a lot better. I released my hair from the shower cap. I wiped my hand across the mirror and stared at my reflection. I still looked like me. Not a vengeful demon, just me. I sighed and brushed my teeth in the hope of ridding myself of a weird metallic taste in my mouth.

My mind wandered to Nikki again. I'll send her a message and check in on her tomorrow. I frowned, I felt a sensation of pressure in my head, not painful just odd. I focused back on my reflection. There was a strange glow in my eyes. I leaned closer to the mirror to examine them. There was a gold ring around the outer section of my iris. As I examined my eyes, the gold-coloured ring around my iris spread outwards like a flare. The colour was so intense it looked like my eyes were illuminated from within. What the hell is it? I closed my eyes, opened them, and blinked repeatedly. It was gone. My familiar amber eyes looked back at me from the mirror. What was that?

I shook my head, bewildered at the experience. I was getting worried that I was either losing my mind or something even worse was happening to me. I left the bathroom and returned to my room. I pulled on some underwear and put on an old T-Shirt and leggings. A feeling of dread was gathering in the pit of my stomach. Something was wrong. I also had a feeling that whatever it was, would result in an irreversible change, and that scared me. So much for maintaining control, I was fraying at the edges. But freaking out about something I couldn't put a label on, would not help me. Get a grip, Brissy!

I had something constructive to focus my agitated mind on. I prepared a new study and revision schedule to ensure that I covered all the topics on my A Level courses. I had to ensure that I had plenty of time to work on and submit my final assignment papers. My exams were in six months. There's still a lot of reading to do for English Literature, my final assignment for Business Studies was due in four weeks, Law in Society was the only subject that was well under control.

My next study and revision session on my schedule starts in fifteen minutes. Plenty of time to pop downstairs and grab a coffee. It would be a gruelling schedule, but I must stick to it to give myself the best chance of success. As I left my room and shut the door behind me, the door opposite mine opened.

"Hi Brissy, haven't seen you all day. How goes it?" Grace's slender form stood in her bedroom doorway. She is tall, only a couple of inches shorter than me. Her delicate features set off by the short, structured bob of her black hair. Grace had a natural classic beauty; she was well named. Although she was only sixteen, she had a poise that was beyond her years.

"Hey. Going down to get a cup of coffee before I start a revision session. What's up?" I gave Grace a smile, my mind was already on the work I needed to do.

"Perfect, can I have five minutes of your time? I need help choosing an outfit for my date." There was a twinkle in her green eyes. "Planning to dazzle Tom tonight. It took him a long time to ask me out." I didn't doubt that Grace would achieve her goal. Tom would indeed be dazzled.

"Let me grab a coffee, I'll be right back. Want one?"

"I'm good, thanks."

"OK, won't be long." I went downstairs into the kitchen. Amada was sitting at the table.

"Hi Amada, how has your day been?" I walked over to her and kissed her on the cheek. She looked up and patted my hand, an affectionate look on her face.

"Hi honey. I take it your study and revision schedule has started?" I nodded, moving to fill up the kettle.

"Yes, I'm just about to start a session. What time are you heading out?" I turned to face Amada whilst waiting for the kettle to boil. Amada is a petite woman in her mid-fifties with honey coloured hair and a kind face. We had a running joke in the house that she was surrounded by giants but ruled the roost. Amada is half Spanish and half English. Our chosen title for her was to pay homage to her Spanish origins. Something that both touched and delighted her and Amado.

"Within the hour, I need to get a move on. I know you will do well Brissy. You always give a hundred percent to your goals." Amada's warm brown eyes showed her pride in me. I gave her a wide smile.

"Can I get you a drink?"

"No, I am fine thanks."

I made my coffee and walked towards the kitchen door. "I'll see you later."

"OK, honey."

I returned upstairs. I tapped on Grace's bedroom door and entered.

"Where is he taking you?" Grace beckoned me over to where she stood in front of her wardrobe. From the state of her room, it looked like half her wardrobe was scattered around it. She turned to face me, an excited look on her face.

"We are going to dinner. He mentioned that the restaurant will also have live music and dancing. He hasn't told me the name of the restaurant. I've narrowed down the options to three outfits." She pointed to a simple long sleeve dress made of black lace mesh with a gold underlay material, it looked about knee length. The second dress was red and sleeveless, the top was made of velvet and the skirt was a pleated chiffon that was calf length. I had seen Grace in the red dress before, she looked great. The third outfit was a black and silver jumpsuit.

"Definitely the red dress. You wore it to Amada's birthday dinner; you looked stunning. Tom will be suitably dazzled, for sure!" Grace laughed and gave me a hug.

"I have just the accessory you need. Give me a second." I dashed to my room and grabbed my drop rose gold love heart earrings. Each earring had three hearts linked vertically. The hearts were set with red stones and tiny black beads. I returned to Grace's room and handed her the earrings.

"Oh Brissy, they're beautiful, and perfect for my dress. Thank you! I'll take good care of them."

"I think you should sleek your hair back. Let those unbelievably high cheek bones of yours stand out. Maybe create a couple of curls near your temple, you know like those twenties' styles."

"I never thought of that, thanks."

"What's Tom like?"

"He's sweet and kind. It's amazing really that a guy so good looking isn't full of himself. I wasn't sure he'd ask me out. Lot of other girls have been trying to catch his attention. He just quietly goes about his way not seeming to notice. I really hope he opens up during dinner. I want to find out what he's really like."

"He sounds great." Grace nodded, a dreamy look on her face.

"He really is."

"Right, my work here is done, have a great night, don't do anything I wouldn't do". I gave her a cheeky wink. She raised an eyebrow and shook her head. I entered my room, closed the door, and sat at my desk. Time to work. I spent forty minutes creating flash cards to cover the topics of corporate structures and directors' duties.

I was shuffling through my newly created flash cards when there was a brief knock and Amada came in. She was dressed in a flattering ankle length black dress.

"Hi honey, are you winning?" Amada smiled as she crossed the room to stand next to my desk. I twisted in my chair to face her giving her a bright smile.

"I got a lot done. I am tired, but glad I can look forward to a relaxing evening. You look lovely, where are you having dinner, and what show are you seeing?"

"We are eating at Moonlights; I have been looking forward to dining there. After dinner, we are off to see what can rightly be described as a classical music extravaganza at the Symphony Hall. It will be a lovely ladies' evening. Val and Aggie are always great company. What are you having for dinner?"

"I am going to oven bake some salmon steaks. Boil some new potatoes and some mixed veg. There is basil and pepper sauce to go with it. For dessert, there is apple tart and ice cream." I rubbed my stomach.

"Lovely, nutritious, tasty and reasonably quick. Time for me to go. Enjoy your evening in. I will be home late; see you in the morning." Amada bent and gave me a hug and left my room.

I stood up and stretched. Felt tired, and not hungry. I lay down on my bed, put my earphones on and played my classical play list. The soothing sound of the flute seeped into my troubled mind. I drew in a deep breath and exhaled through my mouth. My eyes drifted closed. The sound of the music grew fainter.

I was in the warm embrace of a man. I could not see his face even though I was looking up at him. We were in my bedroom standing close to my bed. He bent his head and kissed me deeply. I kissed him back. He let out a deep groan, his hands moved under my jumper and camisole to touch my bare skin. I gasped with pleasure as his hand reached my breast. Dear God, I was on fire. I pulled his T-shirt free from his jeans over his head. He removed my jumper and camisole; we were naked from waist up.

We lay down on my bed, he showered little kisses over my face. His lips move down my neck, shoulders and across my breasts. I moaned with pleasure. His lips returned to mine for another long kiss. He lifted his head slowly looking directly into my eyes with dark warm brown eyes.

"Brissy, I want you." His voice was hoarse with passion. I lifted my head and kissed him.

"God, you are so sweet," he moaned as we broke our kiss for air. My fingers moved over his chest as our lips met again. I wanted him too, I wanted him badly. His hand was on the elastic waistband of my leggings, he slid them down my legs with ease. I let out a gasp as he touched me, I closed my eyes giving in to the pleasure and anticipation. My eyes flickered open again and our eyes met. He gave me another slow kiss. I still could not see his face for some reason, just those dark brown eyes. Yet I felt certain I knew him.

"You are so beautiful, so much more than I imagined." I sensed hesitation in his voice, his eyes were conflicted. He took a deep breath and buried his head in my neck. We lay like that for a while. He finally raised his head and looked at me.

"You're so young, too young!"

"No, I'm not. I'll be nineteen in six months."

"I am older than you so I should damn well know better! I can't make love to you." He got up from the bed and pulled his T-shirt back on. I feel about fifty, even though I am only twenty-two. I have seen too many horrors. I don't want to taint you with my issues, and I have quite a few issues. It is best that we just stay friends."

"No, you are wrong, there is something between us and I want to find out what it is. I know you want to as well." He was standing looking down at me.

"I do. But we can't always have what we want. Sometimes, what we want is just not good for us!" He turned and left my room. I was left with a deep sense of loss.

My eyes slowly fluttered open. I rubbed at my sleepy eyes with both hands and turned to look at my alarm clock, 8:30 PM. Despite the two naps my head still felt groggy, and that metallic taste was back.

I felt uneasy about my dream. Although I hadn't seen the face of the man, I'd been so passionate with, I knew who those dark brown eyes belong to. They were Kade's eyes. What the hell was happening to me? I was having sex dreams about Kade of all people!

If I was honest with myself, I had to admit that I been fascinated with Kade for several years. I remembered the first time I saw him; I was fifteen. My cheeks warmed at the events of that day.

Me and Funmi were attending a friends' birthday party. Marcus dropped me off at Funmi's house. Funmi's mum answered the door and informed me that Funmi was still getting dressed.

I went straight up intending to go into Funmi's bedroom. I decided to quickly use the bathroom. I glimpsed Funmi's dad in the living room on my way upstairs so thought the bathroom was free.

I went into the bathroom without knocking. As I closed the door quietly behind me, the shower curtains were suddenly drawn to reveal a naked man. At first, he didn't see me standing by the closed bathroom door. He opened the plastic storage drawers next to the bath and took out a shower gel. As he straightened, he saw me. I stood there unable to move or speak my eyes about to pop out of my head. He looked like one of those famous Greek nude sculptures of athletes.

He asked who I was, in a deep even voice. He made no attempt to cover himself. His eyes were fixed on my face.

I remember stumbling over my words as I responded and asked who he was. I was so embarrassed, but my feet weren't responding to the signals from my brain.

I still remember that neutral tone as he said it wasn't a good time for introductions. That we could meet and greet at a more appropriate time. There had been a pause whilst he waited for me to leave. I was still rooted to the spot. In a mocking tone, he suggested I leave unless I planned to watch him shower. I finally gathered my wits and fled.

ဆာဢ၆ဢ

5. ENCOUNTER

My thoughts returned to the present. I could feel the tension building up in my body again My head started to ache. I gave a deep sigh. I would have to take each day at a time. Over thinking this muddle was getting me nowhere.

I got up; I still didn't feel particularly hungry. I did not fancy a substantial meal. Some cereal would do fine. The house was quiet. I guess I was home alone. I went down to the kitchen and ate a bowl of cereal. I checked that the patio doors were locked, made myself a chamomile tea and returned to my room.

I placed the cup of tea on my bedside table and paid a quick visit to the bathroom. As I was returning from the bathroom, I thought I heard a faint female voice calling me. I turned around, not expecting anyone to be there, and of course the landing was empty.

On edge and tired, I entered my room. Pulled on my PJs and got into bed; sitting up to drink my tea. My eyes were already heavy with sleep by the time I drank the last swallow. I shimmied down into my bed, pulled the duvet up to my chin and turned the light out. I welcomed sleep with open arms.

I felt so at peace, so relaxed. I was standing in what looked like a meadow, the sun was high overhead. I knew I was asleep. I looked around. Ahead of me, in the distance I saw the figure of a woman. She was too far away for me to see her face, but I could see that she wore some sort of a veil. She was dressed in a flowing red gown. It billowed around her in the warm summer breeze. She waved at me and beckoned for me to come over. I started to run towards her. As I got closer, I could see her more clearly. I still could not see her face. She wore a red veil. The only thing I could see were her eyes. They shone like liquid gold. I slowed my pace and stopped a few yards from her. The gown she was wearing was a sort of kaftan made of silk.

"Welcome, Brissy Jayne Yah. I have been waiting a long time for you. I want to show you something." Her voice was strange. It dawned on me that she was not actually speaking. Her mind was talking directly to mine. I wasn't alarmed, simply curious.

"Who are you, how do you know me?" Her eyes seem to smile at me.

"I have known you all your life Brissy. Walk with me, please." She motioned for us to step onto a white path. The colour was a sharp contrast to the brown earth around it. I followed the path with my eyes and saw that it snaked far ahead until it seemed to merge with the horizon. She stepped onto the path and stood waiting for me to join her.

I hesitated, unsure whether I wanted to join her. I looked down at my feet, I was wearing yellow sandals. I noticed for the first time what I was wearing. I wore the same style of gown as the woman. Mine was yellow, a sort of mustard shade.

"It's your true-life path, Brissy. You must walk it to become who you were born to be." Again, she communicated with me without speaking. I looked up at her. There was encouragement in her gold eyes. I nodded and stepped onto the path with my right foot. My left foot remained on the brown earth next to it. I heard a rumbling sound, it echoed all around us. The air was suddenly very still. It felt like everything around us was frozen. I lifted my left foot and placed it on the path. As soon as my left foot touched the path everything around us started to fold in on itself. Like a piece of paper being folded repeatedly, reducing in size until it vanished entirely. The rumbling sound returned. I should have been afraid, but I wasn't. I glanced at my companion. A cool wind lifted her veil, stripping it off her completely. I watched the wind carry the red veil high into the sky until it was just a red speck. I brought my attention back to her. She too had her head lifted to the sky watching the veil disappear, her back to me. Slowly she turned to face me.

She had my mother's face! Instinctively, I knew she was not my mother. I traced the lines of her face with my eyes. My mother had hazel eyes. Save for the difference in eye colour, she was a younger representation of my mother. Probably as she would have looked, at my age.

"Why do you look like my mother?" She smiled at my question.

"You chose this face for me, Brissy. You can change it if it does not, please you." I frowned at her response. I guess if I was dreaming, I was in control of my dream, at least to a degree.

"This is a dream; I fell asleep in my bed." She nodded at my statement.

"Yes, you are asleep. How do you feel, Brissy?" Her gold eyes watched my face intently.

"I feel …" I was about to say 'fine', but I no longer felt fine. A searing pain spread from my temples to my forehead, then to the back of my head. I fell to my knees holding my head in my hands crying out in pain.

"My head, what's happening to me?" She knelt in front of me her eyes full of empathy.

"I know you are in great pain Brissy, but you must bear it. The awakening is never easy." The pain increased to an unbearable level. My tortured screams echoed all around me, I curled up in a defensive ball still holding my head and continued to scream. It felt like my brain was on fire, and it was melting in the intensity of the heat.

"BJ, wake up, BJ!" Someone was shaking me; my eyes flew open. The first thing I saw was Marcus' concerned face looking down at me. A shaft of light entered my room from the hallway. The pain in my head was gone. Had it even been real or just part of my dream? Marcus turned on my bedside lamp. He looked pale.

Whilst the pain in my head was gone, I felt spent, like someone zapped all the energy out of me. I was still lying down unable to summon the energy to sit up.

"Marcus, help me sit up, please." He helped me to sit up, placing my pillows behind my back. I held his gaze,

"What is it?"

"It's your eyes, BJ. The colour has changed – they are gold. You look different somehow too. Is your sight OK, any blurred vision, headache or nausea?" I shook my head; I technically didn't have a headache now, so it was not a lie.

"Your temperature feels normal, how do you feel? Your screams scared the life out of me. Was it a nightmare that made you scream like that?"

"It was just a bad dream; I am OK now. Sorry, did I wake you?"

"No, I only got home twenty minutes ago. The change in your eye colour is very strange. Maybe we should go to A&E and get you checked out."

"There's no way I am going to spend hours sitting in A&E when I feel fine."

"This isn't normal, BJ."

"Feel fine, just tired. Let's talk about this in the morning."

"It's freaking me out, are you sure you're OK and your vision is, OK?"

"I can see just fine." I didn't tell him about the pain in my head, I kept that to myself. "I feel fine, just tired." I lay back down.

"Call me if you need anything." I nodded. He got up in a fluid motion and stood looking down at me for a moment.

"OK, I hope you can get some sleep, any issues call me."

"Thanks Marcus, good night."

"Good night, BJ," he left my room closing the door quietly behind him.

It was still relatively early. Amada and Grace were clearly not home yet. In fact, I was surprised that Marcus was home. He was usually out most Saturday nights returning in the early hours of Sunday.

I reached for my phone and put the camera in selfie mode. I held it up to my face and gasped. I didn't recognise the eyes looking back at me. They shone like molten gold. I suddenly felt cold. I had seen the same shade of eyes before. I lay very still. After a few minutes I noticed the pain in my palms. My fists were clenched so tightly that my nails were digging into the palms of my hand. I turned off the light and made a conscious effort to relax. Tiredness rose again and I drifted off to sleep.

I found myself standing on the white path again. The collapsed surrounding on either side of the path was vastly different now. I was surrounded by what looked like a magical fairy-tale forest. Everywhere I looked there were beautiful flowers, plants, and birds in vibrant hues of just about every colour I could think of. Water cascaded over rock formations made from what looked like glass. On each side of the path for as far as my eye could see was about a metre strip of copper coloured glass beads.

It was not just my eyes that were given a treat. I could hear beautiful bird song, the sound of rushing water and the gentle movement of the wind through the trees. A combination of lovely scents from the flowers and plants wafted through the air. The experience was like a perfect orchestral composition of nature. I felt so alive. Free like a weight was lifted off me.

My mind felt incredibly agile, like I could solve the most challenging mathematical equation in the blink of an eye. I looked down at my feet on the path, I was wearing sandals in a delicate pale blue. My eyes moved up my body to see what I was wearing. My gown was the same style as the yellow one but this time the colour was pale blue like my sandals. My hair moved in the gentle breeze.

At equal distances along both sides of the path there were yellow wooden benches. I walked to the bench closest to me, sat down on it and waited for her. She materialised out of thin air on the bench opposite me, she was wearing a white gown. I looked into her gold eyes; it was like looking into my own unrecognisable eyes.

"Hello again, I have lots of questions for you." I didn't speak, my mind communicated directly with her mind. She smiled.

"Hello, Brissy, it's good to see you awake." I knew I was still asleep and dreaming.

"What is the awakening?"

"The awakening is what can best be described as the point when dormant parts of your brain fire back into life. They wake up. It is a painful but necessary process for your mind to accommodate your developing capabilities."

"Will I have to feel that horrible pain again?" She hesitated before responding.

"The probability is that you will not feel the pain of the awakening again. However, there are multiple levels of awakening. But I am not aware of any person reaching the second level." I was relieved to hear that the chances of me feeling the pain of the awakening again was close to zero.

"What is your name?" I cannot keep referring to her as the woman or my companion. She must have a name.

"I do not have a name. You may give me one if you wish."

"It feels like you are more than my imagination, who or what are you?"

"I am a manifestation of your mind. I am another side of you; yet separate from you."

"You have been communicating directly with my mind and have not said a single word yet. Can you speak?" She nodded and spoke.

"Yes Brissy. I can speak but the best way for us to communicate is through a cerebral connection. You need to practice your new capabilities. That is how I will communicate with you. Please do the same. It may feel a little strange at first. But the more you practise the capability, it will become as familiar to you as breathing." Her voice was light and pleasant. She looked around and smiled.

"You have a wonderful imagination, this is beautiful. Everything you see, including me, is created by your mind."

"Thank you. I think you should have a name. How do you like Soraya?" It was the name of a character from one of my favourite books as a child. About a celestial princess. She laughed.

"As in the Pleiades stars cluster. I like it – Soraya it is. Your mind needs rest. I will see you in your sleep tomorrow night."

"Please wait, can you tell me why my eye colour has changed? It looks like yours now. Is there something wrong with me?"

"No, Brissy. There is nothing wrong with you. The change in your eye colour is a side effect of what you are going through. I will tell you more tomorrow night, you must rest now." She disappeared before I could ask my next question.

I woke up with a start. I remembered every detail of my encounter with Soraya. It was clearly not time to get up yet. My gaze moved to my alarm clock; 3:00 AM. Determined to claim my remaining hours of sleep, I closed my eyes and attempted to empty my mind.

I was in an empty cinema watching a black and white film of what looked like one of my family gatherings. We were all there, including Amado. It was Amada's last birthday celebration with Amado. He kissed Amada on the cheek and presented her with a ring box. Her face radiated with happiness. She opened the box, gasped, and threw her arms around Amado in delight. They hugged rocking back and forth. When their embrace ended, Amado took the ring out of the box. It was a beautiful diamond eternity ring with a heart shaped centre stone. He slid the ring onto Amada's finger and gave her a kiss. Amada raised her hand to admire her new ring. The ring slowly faded until it was gone. A shadow of sorrow settled on Amada's face. Her eyes darted to Amado, she reached for him. Her hand went right through his image. His hands reached for her, but they could not touch as Amado's image faded. Tears rolled down Amada's eyes. She covered her face with both her hands and wept.

I woke up slowly, stretching under my duvet. I felt a lot better, the tiredness was gone, my mind felt sharp and clear. A feeling of sadness hovered over me. I caught a whiff of coffee and turned in the direction of the aroma. Marcus was sitting at my desk watching me, a mug of coffee in his hand.

"Good morning, did you sleep well? You look a lot better, how are you feeling?" I glanced at my alarm clock – 8:15 AM. I sat up in bed and smiled.

"I feel great, thanks. How long have you been sitting there?"

"About fifteen minutes or so." Marcus shook his head frowning.

"What?"

"Still can't get over your new eye colour."

"Does it look weird?" I watched him carefully

"Let's just say it's very unusual. It calls attention to your face."

"Attention is something I don't need or want."

"Well, it looks like you won't have much say in that. You need to see the doctor about it. If you won't go to A&E, you have to call the surgery and make an appointment tomorrow."

"I can see you won't let this go. Fine, I will go and see the doctor."

"Amada will have something to say about it too. I'll make us scrambled eggs."

"Thanks. A quick shower, then I'll be down."

Marcus nodded and left. I jumped out of bed feeling energetic. I quickly stripped off my clothes and put on my robe. I left my room pulling the door closed behind and went into the bathroom. I decided to wash my hair. I grabbed my shampoo and entered the shower. I increased the temperature of the water. I allowed the water to saturate my hair, poured some shampoo into my palm and rubbed it through my hair working the lather from the roots to the ends. I rinsed and washed it a second time, then quickly scrubbed down my body with my sponge. My skin was tingling and warm. I stayed under the jets of water for a couple more minutes, then stepped out of the shower. I wrapped my body with a thick towel and wrapped a smaller towel around my hair.

The bathroom was warm and steamy. I wiped my hand across the mirror. It felt odd as I gazed into my own eyes, not recognising them. I now know what Marcus meant; my face looked different. But I couldn't tell exactly what else had changed. My skin had a warm glow to it.

I brushed my teeth, staring at my reflection and let my mind wander. The words "eternity ring" sprang into my mind. I remembered my dream.

As I dressed, I saw a sudden image of Amada's eternity ring. This new turn of having weird random thoughts and feelings, the change in my eye colour, not to mention Carl, were beginning to freak me out! I hoped that there was an explanation for the occurrences, that was benign. One that did not involve me losing my mind.

There is nothing wrong with you. You are becoming more of yourself. You will understand soon enough. I almost jumped out of my skin. Those words popped into my mind, but it felt like someone responded to my thoughts. Soraya? I felt a sudden calm.

Half an hour later, I leaned back in my chair surveying what was left of my breakfast, which was not much at all. I took a sip of my coffee.

"Thanks, Marcus. I didn't realise how hungry I was." I patted my stomach. "Have you seen Amada this morning?"

"No, but I heard her going up to her room as I was returning from my run. She was muttering something to herself."

"I'm going to take a mug of coffee up to her, I'll see you later."

"I will do the dishes."

"Thanks." I left the kitchen with Amada's coffee in hand avoiding Marcus' eyes. I made my way up to Amada's room. Taking care not to spill the coffee, I climbed the stairs to the second floor of the house. I knocked on her door.

"Come in." A couple of steps into Amada's room I stopped. My eyes widened as I looked around the room. Amada didn't look up from the drawer she was rummaging through.

"Good morning, honey." She had her back to me. I wondered how she knew it was me? She straightened and turned towards me. She made her way over to me, her progress across the room interrupted as she picked up various obstacles in her path. Her eyes met mine for the first time since I arrived. Her eyes widened.

"Brissy, what is going on with your eye colour, are you wearing contact lenses?" She frowned. I took a deep silent breath and responded in a casual tone.

"No, my eye colour randomly changed. I am fine, there is nothing wrong with my vision and I already know what you are going to say. I will call the surgery tomorrow for an appointment to see the doctor." She was now standing in front of me examining my eyes up close.

"That is very strange, are you sure you feel, OK?" I nodded. "The colour is unusual, it's gold. I have never heard of anyone's eye colour changing so drastically. I will come to the doctor with you tomorrow." I knew she would not take 'no' for an answer. Relieved she did not insist I go to A&E; I didn't bother trying to dissuade her. I looked around her room.

"What's going on?" I asked, waving at the mess in her room as I handed her the coffee. She took a sip.

"Thanks, honey. I think I have lost my eternity ring; it was the last gift Amado gave me. I have turned my room upside down; I cannot find it anywhere. I noticed it was missing on my way home last night. I was hoping and praying that I left it at home, I have been searching for it all morning." I steadied myself – Amada's eternity ring was lost. It was gone like in my dream. I cleared my throat.

"Did you check with the restaurant whether anyone handed it in?"

"The restaurant is not open yet; they open at 11:30 AM. I am going to go there. If they don't have it, I will have to go to the Symphony Hall and check with them." Amada's voice wobbled and tears started to well up in her eyes.

"I will go with you. But first, let's go for a walk, some fresh air will be good for both of us."

"That's a good idea. I will meet you downstairs in ten minutes. Thanks, honey." I squeezed her shoulder.

"I have a good feeling we'll find your ring, see you in a few minutes."

I returned to my room. Put some lip gloss on my lips and swept my hair up in a knot on top of my head. I sent Nikki a text message to let her know that I would be popping in to see her later. Once we find Amada's ring, I'll go and see her. I paused; I hoped we would find Amada's ring. But I couldn't be sure we would, or did I know something that I didn't know? I shook my head at the confusing train of thoughts and went downstairs.

Marcus was still in the kitchen, reading the newspaper.

"Marcus, Amada has lost her eternity ring. I'm going to go into town with her to help her to check with the restaurant she was at last night." Marcus looked up, a frown on his face.

"That's not good. Do you need any help?"

"The two of us should be able to handle it. The restaurant is not open yet; we are going for a walk first. See you later."

"OK, good luck." I went into the hallway and met Amada coming down the stairs.

"Brissy, perfect timing, are you ready to head out?" Amada was more like her usual self although sadness still lingered in her eyes. I nodded and pulled on my coat and handed her coat to her.

"OK, let's go, it's been a while since the two of us walked in Cannon Hill Park. We will be able to walk for a good half hour before we have to go to the restaurant."

We left and got into Amada's red Nissan Micra.

ဆၢလ်ဆၢ

6. INTUITION

"It's such a lovely bright day, perfect for a walk." I made small talk with Amada as she drove the few minutes to the park. We arrived to find a busy carpark. We managed to find an empty bay some distance from the entrance of the park. Amada paid for the parking and we walked towards the park entrance. I hooked my arm through Amada's as we entered. We walked in silence for about five minutes.

"How was the concert last night?" I broke the silence. She launched into an enthusiastic account of her evening of classical music. I provided the right prompts on cue to encourage her to continue talking. I looked around as we walked, it was busy, the gorgeous day enticed a lot of people to get out. I took a deep breath of fresh air. Feeling grateful despite the recent events and additions to my challenges. I reminded myself of the comforting saying that my mother was fond of. 'God never gives us more than we can handle'. I believed it, and that gave me courage. Someone was calling Amada's name.

"Claire, Claire Morgan?" Amada and I turned in the direction of the female voice. A woman walking a lively Cocker Spaniel waved at us as she approached. I glanced at Amada. There was recognition on her face. She smiled at the woman and waved back. Amada stepped towards the approaching woman. I released her arm and hung back.

"Martha, what a lovely surprise, it has been years. How are you?" There was an echo of familiarity about the woman. Amada and the woman shook hands and chatted excitedly. They both headed back in my direction. The woman's eyes were fixed on my face. She looked at me as if she were searching for something.

"Brissy, do you remember Martha Maddison?" I shook my head giving them a rueful smile. Martha moved closer to me, a warm smile on her face. Her blue eyes continued to probe my face.

"Hello, Brissy, its lovely to see you again. What a beautiful young woman you have grown into! Your eyes are even more striking than I remember. I was your therapist for a few months after you joined Claire's family." Strange, I still couldn't remember her.

"Hello, Ms Maddison." She laughed as her Cocker Spaniel jumped up at my leg.

"Behave yourself, Pendle. Sorry, he is very excitable. Please call me Martha." I bent down and stroked Pendle's soft glossy fur. Martha and Amada chatted for a bit. Apparently, Martha and her husband had been abroad for five years. I studied Martha. There was something in the recess of my mind about her, but I couldn't get to it. She invited Amada for a coffee sometime to catch-up. Amada accepted her invitation, and they exchanged numbers. She turned to me.

"It was nice to see you again, Brissy, take care of yourself." Her words were casual, but I detected something else in her tone. She turned to address Amada, "I will contact you in a couple of weeks Claire, so we can set a date to meet up. Enjoy the rest of the weekend."

"That will be great, I look forward to it. Bye, Martha." She pulled at Pendle's leash and gave us a wave and walked off in the opposite direction to us. I checked the time on my phone, it was 11:15 AM.

"Time for us to head back Amada, it's 11:15 AM." I hooked my arm through Amada's again and we retraced our steps. I glanced sideways at Amada as we walked back to the entrance of the park. She looked better. There was a rosy glow in her cheeks from the cold winter air. I felt calmer too. The walk had done us both good.

"What a timely coincidence that we saw Martha today. She would be the perfect option for your counselling sessions after your exams. She got to know you well when you were younger. The social worker mentioned that you seemed to connect with her more than other counsellors that you saw. I will send you, her details."

"How long did I see her for?" It was strange that I still could not remember my sessions with Martha.

"You saw her once a week for a good six months or so. She stopped seeing you because her husband got a job offer in the US. The sessions with her really seemed to help you. I thought she was something of a miracle worker. I would drop you off at the sessions, Grace and I would go shopping. Marcus insisted on sitting in the waiting room – waiting for you. She helped you a lot. Why do you ask?"

"I just think it's strange that I don't remember her."

I racked my brain trying to remember Martha but there was nothing other than the echo of the familiarity of her face. I knew there were many things about the period between my mother's death and the first three to four years afterwards that I did not remember. Either my memory was sketchy, or it was a complete blank. I guess Martha is one of my buried memories. We exited the park and made our way back to the car.

It only took us ten minutes to get to the city centre. We found parking near the restaurant. Moonlights is one of the new restaurants that popped up in the newly refurbished buildings in the city centre. Over the last three years or so the whole vibe of the city centre changed. A wide variety of good restaurants to fit any palate and price range sprung up. The regeneration phase of the city centre that had been completed was a great success, and there was much more to come. Everything you could wish for in terms of entertainment, dining, bars, museums and galleries, and city living, were within an easy distance. Everything was easy to access on foot and the quality of what was on offer was great. This is another one of the many things I love about Birmingham.

At exactly 11:30 AM we were approaching the restaurant. A waiter was unlocking the doors as we reached the entrance. He opened the door and let us in.

"Good morning, is it a table for two you need?" The waiter greeted us with a smile.

"Good morning, we are here about a ring I lost last night. I had dinner here last night, I was wondering whether anyone found my ring and handed it in." There was a hopeful look on Amada's face as she spoke.

"I can certainly find out for you, one moment please." The waiter went to the bar to speak to a man dressed in a suit. I had a sudden feeling that we should visit the Ladies before we leave the restaurant.

"Did you use the Ladies' last night?" I didn't need to go, so I assumed the urge I felt that we should both visit the Ladies was some sort of vibe related to Amada's ring.

"Yes, a couple of times, do you think maybe I dropped my ring in there?"

"If the waiter tells us that no one has handed it in, I will ask him if we can use the facilities before we go. We can have a quick look around." Amada nodded in agreement. The waiter was walking back towards us.

"I am terribly sorry Madam, no one handed in a ring last night." His tone was sympathetic. Disappointment was written all over Amada's face.

"Thank you. Do you mind if we use the Ladies' before we leave?" I patted Amada's back as I spoke.

"Yes, of course, it's just through there to your left." He indicated the direction with his hand.

"Thank you." I put an arm around Amada's shoulder and guided her in the direction given. When we entered the Ladies', I turned to Amada.

"Do you remember which cubicles you used last night?" Amada nodded. There was a dejected look on her face. She was steeling herself for the possibility that her ring may not be found.

"It was these two," Amada pointed to the two end cubicles opposite each other.

"OK, you take a look in that one, I'll look in this one." We entered the cubicles, I took a thorough look around, no ring. As I was about to exit the cubicle, I saw a flash of light from the drain on the floor. I bent down for a closer look. I could see it clearly now; it was Amada's ring.

"Amada, I sort of found your ring." I was praying that we would be able to get it out without it falling further down the drain. Amada rushed in her face bright with hope.

"Where is it, and what do you mean by, you sort of found it?" I pointed down at the drain. Amada bent to inspect the drain. She gasped.

"I see it, Brissy, I see it! Oh, you wonderful girl, you found it!" I frowned, trying to manage her jubilation.

"We still have to get it out safely. You stay here while I go and get assistance. Don't try and fish it out, it could fall further down the drain." Amada nodded; her eyes still fixed on the drain. I hurried to find the waiter. He was standing by the bar.

"Excuse me. We found my foster mum's ring. It has fallen down the drain in one of the cubicles in the Ladies. We need help getting it out." The waiter looked at me in surprise then delight at the prospects of a happy ending.

"Yes Madam, let's see what we can do to get it out. Let me take a look first." He followed me back. Amada was standing over the drain as if she were guarding it. She came out of the cubicle so the waiter could look.

"Yes, I see it. We should have a screwdriver that we can use to remove the drain cap. I don't want to attempt to fish it out in case it falls further down the drain." I nodded in agreement.

"I'll be right back." He left to find a screwdriver for the job. Amada paced up and down a worried look on her face. The waiter returned holding a screwdriver accompanied by one of his colleagues.

I walked over to Amada and steered her away from the cubicle to where the hand dryers were. We stood in silence and left the waiters to it, hoping for the best. Five minutes or so later the waiter I asked for assistance approached us with a big smile on his face. He held a tissue in his partially closed hand. When he reached us, he held out his hand and unwrapped the object in the tissue. Amada's beautiful eternity ring lay there, the diamonds twinkling, none the worse for wear. Amada shrieked and held out her hand, tears rolling down her cheeks.

"Thank you so much! This ring is very precious to me, I can't thank you enough." I smiled at the waiter; his colleague joined us.

"Thanks for your help, we really appreciate it." My eyes flicked to their name badges – Alfredo and Luke.

"We are delighted that the ring has been found and that we could help," said Luke. Alfredo nodded a happy smile on his face. I gave them both a grateful smile and turned to hug Amada.

"We will be on our way shortly." Amada said.

"There is no rush, Madam." Luke said giving Amada an understanding look. They smiled and left. I smiled at Amada.

"I told you I had a good feeling we would find your ring. It's wonderful that you have it back. I know how much it means to you."

"I would never have found it without you, Brissy. Thank you so much. Your level of intuition has always amazed me, thank you, honey." She gave me a tight hug. "Let me mop up my face and we can leave."

A few minutes later, we conveyed our thanks again to Luke and Alfredo and left the restaurant. I caught a glimpse of the clock as we left. It was 11:50 AM.

"Shall we have lunch in town to celebrate?" Amada asked.

"I am guessing you didn't sleep well last night. I think you should head home and relax, maybe take a nap. I am going to see Nikki. I'll walk from here, it's not far. I will be home by 3:00 PM. I am scheduled to work on my Business Studies assignment."

"You are right. I did not sleep well last night; I am just beginning to realise that I am tired. Thanks again, honey." She gave me a hug.

"See you later." I waved goodbye as I started walking towards the Jewellery Quarter.

I wondered whether Nikki would have news about Carl's condition. I steeled myself for what was likely to be a difficult conversation. I knew that Nikki would want to go over the events of yesterday in some detail, trying to understand what happened.

I tripped and fell forward. A pair of hands steadied me saving me from falling flat on my face. I looked up to meet curious bright blue eyes.

"Thank you. I should have been looking where I was going." My words gushed out.

"My pleasure. I never pass up an opportunity to save a beautiful woman. Are you OK?" There was a hint of an accent I couldn't place.

"I am fine, thanks." I cringed inside; it could have been worse.

"Bart, she is clearly fine, I think you can let go of her arms now." The cutting voice came from behind me. He slowly released my arms and looked over my shoulder. I turned around to see the owner of the razor voice.

A woman was standing by the open door of an expensive looking sports car, a few yards from us. Her outfit screamed designer brand.

"We don't have time for you to pursue your exotic taste right now, let's go!" Her voice was insulting, and it was clear from her expression that she intended to cause offense. There was a scornful look in her blue eyes as she looked me up and down.

"Please excuse my sister. We were taught good manners; she was not a good student. Have a good day and do take care." There was amusement in his voice. He nodded, walked to the car, his long strides eating up the distance.

He got in the driver side, she got in too, I watched them drive off.

What a bitch! I felt fleeting sympathy for Bart. He probably apologised a lot for his rude sister. I also detected a detestable undertone when she used the word 'exotic'. My colour was something I did not want to define me; it was simply part of who I was. I tried not to relate unpleasant events to the colour of my skin. I hated ever having to arrive at the conclusion – it is because I am black.

It once took a lot of effort to mould my mind to not focus on colour whether it was my own or that of those I encountered. Now, my mind operated on semi auto pilot, until there was a trigger that linked my experience to something unpleasant in the past. The term exotic was one of those trigger words.

Over the years I had long discussions with Funmi about race and equality. I wanted to believe that most people will judge us by our capabilities and contribution, and not by our colour. That was my starting point until I could not find a plausible explanation to explain the actions of others. Funmi's view was, as she called it, more realistic. She agreed that most people were not racist. But she was aware of unconscious bias which often led to discrimination. The things that each of us do unknowingly that can result in detriment to others. The more we are alive to our biases, the better placed we are to avoid discrimination in any respect. We are all wired to be biased in one way or another. It's a lifelong learning journey to recognise and manage our biases.

She made the point that to ignore race, results in a failure to evaluate people as individuals. Each of us were made up of the sum of all our experiences in life. If an individual belongs to a minority group, then their ethnicity would play a part in who they are. There should be recognition of that fact. Her motto was, 'be colour aware not colour blind'.

She was far braver than me when it came to issues of race. But I evaluated her position with an open mind, and sometimes conceded that there was merit in what she said. I gained more balance with my race and heritage over the years. Landing in the position that I am who I am. The judgments and biases of other people is not in my power to control. My goal is to avoid being damaged by negative behaviour, and to try not to accept the unacceptable.

I was approaching Nikki's house; the next couple of hours or so would be interesting. I rang the doorbell, calling on my control to dim the anxiety I felt. Nikki opened the door, looking serious but otherwise normal.

"Hi Brissy – what the … Why is your eye colour different, are you wearing contact lenses?" I was tempted to lie.

"No, I woke up with my eyes this colour. I am going to pay a visit to the doctor tomorrow."

"Goodness, that's strange. The colour is different, it changes your face somehow." Nikki cocked her head to one side as she studied my eyes.

"Are you going to let me in?"

"Sorry, I got distracted by your mesmerising eyes. Come in, I am glad you are here." She pulled me into the house and gave me a hug.

"How are you doing?"

"Not bad. I have some good news about Carl. His mum sent a message, he's going to be OK." I was relieved. "Let's go into the living room, I am home alone." I followed Nikki through the narrow hallway with pale eggshell walls into the sunlit living room and sat next to her on a large cream leather sofa. The walls were a continuation of the pale eggshell shade from the hallway. The room was decorated simply with a distinct sense of order in its presentation. An oak dining table with four matching chairs stood in one corner of the room. The strong colours in the room were provided by the vase of red Carnations on the table and the black glossy piano in the other corner of the room. Nikki's mum is a music teacher. Nikki is a good player, though she took a light-hearted approach to playing. Marsha on the other hand, was turning out to be something of a little prodigy. She loved to play and loved having an audience. We turned to face each other.

"Carl is awake, and the doctors think he will be OK. They are still not sure exactly why he had a fit. But all the tests' results are showing up as normal. His mum suggested I go and see him. I think I'll feel better if I see him. I haven't changed my mind about breaking up with him. We are done, for sure. I just want to see him looking normal to get the horrible images out of my head. Will you come to the hospital with me? Visiting hours start about now. I promise we won't stay long."

I don't want to see Carl. But I understood Nikki's point about the last images of him. Perhaps if I saw him, I too would feel better about the whole thing.

"OK, let's go and see Carl." She reached for my hand and squeezed it.

"Thanks."

Unlike me, Nikki drives and has an old beetle called Faith. Nikki picked up the gift bag that Carl brought that I left on the hall table. It still had the perfume and what was left of his phone in it. She placed it in her big shoulder bag and picked up her keys.

I fiddled with the radio as we drove to the QE Hospital, settling on a station playing Pop music.

"I could really do with a holiday. I feel like getting away for a long weekend. It's my birthday in two weeks, what do you think of a weekend getaway? I'll invite Funmi and Khadijah too." Nikki cast a quick glance my way.

"I am low on cash right now – I can't afford it." I was being careful with money, making a big effort to save.

"That's the great thing about it. My aunt is going to Spain for a couple of weeks on 25 November. She offered me her flat. She lives in a lovely little cottage a short distance from the city centre in York. It shouldn't cost each of us more than £125 for three nights. It will cover the cost of petrol, food, and a bit of entertainment. It would be good for us all to get away."

The idea was tempting, I could manage £125 from my savings.

"It does sound wonderful, OK, count me in." The idea of getting away immediately lifted my mood. It would be my first visit to the walled city. I hoped that Funmi and Khadijah could make it. It was over a year since we all went away together. Nikki turned into the hospital.

"Carl's mum's message said Car Park A is the closest to the ward. Keep an eye out for the sign." Nikki drove slowly as we scanned for the car park sign. "I see it," she said. She drove in and took a ticket. My level of unease was rising as we got closer to seeing Carl. We found the ward easily, a few yards from the entrance, I turned to Nikki.

"Are you sure you want me to come in with you?"

"Yes. Hopefully, he is not going to misbehave, and it will be a dignified short conversation. But I wouldn't put anything past him. Come on, we will be in and out." She took me by the wrist and pulled me along with her. We entered the ward and stood in the entrance looking for Carl.

"He's in the bed at the end," whispered Nikki. She marched forward pulling me along.

Carl's head was turned in the opposite direction to our approach. We stopped at the end of his bed.

"Hello, Carl. You look like you are on the mend," said Nikki. I saw Carl's body stiffen. He turned to look at us and slowly sat up. He looked pale and somehow smaller like he shrunk.

"Nikki, you came, thank you." His voice was hoarse, he gave me a blank look and a brief smile. "Who is your friend?"

"What do you mean? You know Brissy."

Carl shook his head.

"No. I would remember those amazing eyes." Nikki and I exchanged looks.

"Did your doctor say anything about you suffering memory loss?"

"No, there is nothing wrong with my memory."

"Well, I can tell you that you do know Brissy. She is my best friend, and she was with me when you had your fit." Carl scowled. He turned his attention back to me. It was clear from the expression on his face that he genuinely didn't know me.

"Well, Carl, I am glad that you are doing well ... mostly any way. You should mention to your doctor that you have some memory loss." Nikki pulled the gift bag containing the perfume and Carl's scattered phone from her handbag and set it down on his bedside stand. "This belongs to you. I hope you get discharged soon. I won't be visiting again. Goodbye, Carl." Pain flickered across Carl's face.

"Nikki, please wait. I know I treated you badly. What I did is hard to forgive, but I do love you. I just don't know what comes over me sometimes that I get so jealous. I want you to know that I wouldn't have posted the video and it was only on my phone, I didn't save it anywhere else. I am so sorry, Nikki." Nikki searched Carl's face. As far as I could tell, he seemed sincere. I think Nikki came to the same conclusion.

"You need to get help Carl. The next time you lose it, you may go too far and really hurt the woman you are with. Maybe even worse. I love you too. But I love myself more, and I choose myself over you. I'm not going to carry this stuff with me. I don't want to be messed up by the experience with you. I wish you well Carl. Think about what I said and get help." She nodded, turned around and walked away. I cast Carl one last glance; my eyes met his. There was not the slightest flicker of recognition. I followed Nikki out of the ward.

Nikki was silent on the drive back, her face a neutral mask. I knew this was hard for her, she was hurting. Her hands trembled slightly on the steering wheel.

"Can you pull over? I need to pop into the shop for a few things." I motioned for her to pull into the carpark of a small supermarket we were approaching. She nodded and pulled in.

"I won't be long. Can I get you anything?" She gave me a weak smile.

"I'm fine, thanks." I got out of the car and went into the supermarket. I quickly filled my basket with the items I needed, paid, and returned to the car.

"That was quick. What did you buy?"

"Just a few bits for our lunch. Let's go."

Ten minutes later we entered Nikki's kitchen. Much like other parts of Nikki's house it was meticulously tidy. It was not a big room, but the space was well used. I placed my shopping bag on the work surface and unpacked the content. Nikki went to the sink and filled a glass with water. She turned around to face me still wearing the neutral mask. She took small sips of the water.

"Right, we are having ciabatta and tomato toastie with a sprinkle of basil. For dessert, I am making my speciality." I swept my hand across the ingredients for our dessert. Nikki's face lit up.

"Is it…"

"Yep, my creation – Evil Pudding!" We shouted the words out at the same time and laughed.

"Perfect! An overdose of sugar and lots of calories is exactly what I need right now. You make the Evil Pudding. I'll sort out the ciabatta toasties." She turned on the radio. Cold Play's Yellow blared out. We swayed to the music as we made lunch.

I grabbed two dessert bowls. I cut the millionaire's shortbread into small chunks. Cut up some brownies and placed a portion of brownies in each dessert bowl. Then I squirted a generous amount of toffee sauce over the brownie pieces. I spooned clotted cream over the sauce covered brownies. A layer of the millionaire's shortbread pieces followed. Next came the hazel nut chocolate spread, I added two tablespoons to each dessert bowl. More clotted cream went on, topped with a handful of chocolate-covered honeycomb pieces. I finished with a drizzle of salted caramel sauce. I stood back to admire my masterpiece.

Nikki removed the ciabatta and tomato toasties from the grill. I placed the evil puddings in the fridge together with the leftover clotted cream. I put what remained of the ingredients in the cupboard and wiped down the worktop with a damp cloth.

"OK. My creations are chilling nicely in the fridge."

"Good timing, the toasties are ready. Can you grab the apple juice and a couple of glasses? I'll take our plates to the table."

"Sure." I switched the radio off and headed to the living room with the apple juice and glasses. I took the seat opposite Nikki at the table.

"The toasties look yummy. Nicely browned, just the way I like it. Thanks." I poured the juice and moved one of the glasses to Nikki's side of the table.

"Tuck in." I took a bite.

"Delicious! I am really looking forward to a change of scenery. Getting excited about the trip to York."

"Me, too. I will send Funmi and Khadijah a message later today." We ate in silence for a while. "What do you think our lives will be like in five or even ten years from now?" I gave Nikki a surprised look. Swallowed the food in my mouth.

"Life is a contradiction. It's more complicated and simpler than we realise. I know it may not make sense, but that's how I feel. None of us really know what's in store for us. We should try and focus on the people, and things that make us happy."

"Brissy the wise! That sounds way too deep for an eighteen-year-old." She laughed. "I don't know why I am focusing on the future; it will arrive soon enough. I will grab the Evil Pudding and make us coffee, you stay put."

"Thanks." I watched Nikki exit the living room with our empty plates. I leaned back in my chair, suddenly feeling tired. Dwelling on what the future holds is the last thing I want to do. Nikki reappeared carrying a tray with the Evil Puddings and coffee.

"I am going to take your advice. I'll focus on the people and things that make me happy." She announced as she set the tray down on the table. A wide smile curved her lips as she slid back into her seat. "What's that Latin phrase about seizing the day?"

"Carpe Diem."

"Yes, that's it. Carpe Diem – it will be my new motto. Let's talk about you, more to the point, you and Kade. Tell me about the day you met him."

"Can't we talk about something more neutral? Besides, you already know the story."

"Humour me." If it helped to distract Nikki from her pain, it was the least I could do.

"It was the night of Steph's fifteenth birthday party. Marcus dropped me off at Funmi's house. I decided to use the bathroom on my way to Funmi's room. I walked in on Kade; he was about to take a shower. It was horribly embarrassing, and you know the rest. Actually, something funny did happen afterwards."

"Spill it."

I laughed. "I learned about 'the expo test' from Funmi's mum. After the bathroom incident, I was so flustered, and felt such a fool. I just wanted to get out of there before I had to face Kade again. When I told Funmi what happened she teased me horribly. We went to the living room to say goodbye to Funmi's folks." Nikki struggled to stifle her amusement.

"Oh, shut up! It was so embarrassing. Funmi's mum came in, she looked at me and Funmi. Her eyes lingered on Funmi's outfit. I was too distracted to notice what Funmi was wearing. I looked at her outfit too. Funmi's mum says, 'Funmi my dear, are you sure you are ready to go out?' Her tone is casual, Funmi had no clue what was coming but I got the gist of it after seeing Funmi's skirt. Her mum walked over to us; she examined Funmi's face and says, 'your face is as pretty as a picture.' Funmi smiled, still oblivious to what was coming next. Her mum continues 'you appear to have grown since you last wore that skirt.'

Funmi gets a little defensive, she says 'it's a bit short but all essentials are covered.' Her mum smiles and says 'is that so? I wonder whether all essentials will remain covered?' Funmi's mum comes to stand next to me, a few steps behind Funmi. She continues, 'it is always a good idea to do an expo test with short skirts. Bend over and touch your toes.' Funmi bent over, I clapped my hand over my mouth. Her mum keeps a straight face and says, 'my dear, the skirt failed the expo test, your knickers and yash are on view when you bend over.' Nikki laughed so hard tears were running down her face.

"Her bum was out!"

"Yep!" I laughed too; the story never gets old.

"I wish I had been there to witness it first-hand. I can imagine Funmi's face. I take it she was persuaded to change her skirt."

"Yeah! She changed into a less revealing skirt that looked great on her. I love aunty Bola, Funmi is lucky to have her as a mum. Uncle Jacob is pretty cool too." By invitation I addressed Funmi's mum and dad as aunty and uncle. Funmi's parents are from Nigeria. They made a point of sharing stories with me about my father's nation. I had grown close to them over the years and felt relaxed in their company and home. "Right, time to do an evil deed, let's eat the Evil Pudding." We both ate a spoonful and sighed.

"This pudding may be evil by name, but it tastes like heaven." Nikki said as she savoured the taste. She looked visibly more relaxed with a spark of her usual carefree attitude. We continued to reminisce about funny events from our school days.

ಜಂಬಜು

7. REKINDLING

It felt good to be home. I took off my coat and went into the kitchen.

"Hi Grace, how was your date with Tom last night?"

Grace was filling up the kettle, she looked up, her eyes widened as she met my gaze.

"What on earth, your eye colour is different!" I sighed mentally; here we go again…

"Yes, it is. Can I have a cup of coffee please? I don't know how or why the colour has changed. I am going to see the doctor tomorrow." Grace raised her hands in a defensive gesture.

"I guess I am not the first person to ask you about the change in your eye colour. It makes your face come alive," she gave me a sideways look, "there is a sexy edginess to them." I burst out laughing at her words, she smiled.

"You'll see. You are going to see a change in the behaviour of men around you. You are gorgeous, of course. But you've always gone out of your way to understate your looks and body. Now your eyes are going to wrestle that control from you. They command attention."

"Oh Grace, I do love you. Thank you for providing me with some much-needed amusement."

"What's been making you feel so serious? Where've you been?"

"Let's just say it has been an interesting day so far. Tell me about your date with Tom."

Grace gave an excited account of her date. It was clear she was smitten with Tom. I listened with half an ear; my mind strayed to Carl. I felt like I reached a crossroad and whichever path I took; it would take me to an unpredictable destination. I had a sinking feeling that my life was no longer on the course I planned. There was nothing I could do to course correct to get back on the route I wanted to take. I needed solitude.

"I can see that you are somewhat smitten with Tom." I gave Grace a teasing smile. "'I'm glad you had a good night. I have a study session; I'll see you later."

"Here's your coffee, tiger eyes."

"Wolf. My mother used to say I have Wolf eyes. Thanks, see you later." I took my cup of coffee and left the kitchen.

I felt a sense of relief as I entered my room and shut the door behind me. I sat at my desk and drank my coffee. I opened my laptop and played Vivaldi's Four Seasons. The lilting sounds of the violin soothed my jagged nerves.

I started writing my Business Studies paper. My mind was filled with the structure of the paper. I typed away furiously for over two hours. Then relaxed back in my chair, casting a critical eye over the results of my labour. Something was missing, it didn't feel like I quite nailed the question. I would have to do more research using case studies.

My brain seemed to have given a 'stay calm' command. I didn't feel like myself on one level. It felt like I was being introduced to a hidden part of me. My mother. I rarely thought about her, yet over the last few days, she was not far from my thoughts. For over nine years I had not thought about her as much as I have in the last few days. The questions that I have never asked myself were now coming to the forefront of my mind. What happened to her, how did she died? Where was she buried? I was told that my mother had been killed during what they believed was a robbery. There was some sort of explosion that severely damaged parts of the house. My bedroom survived untouched. I'd been too young to digest or question any of the facts of the case. I simply shut down that part of my brain. Now, something had woken it up. I want to know what happened to my mother.

I was in our house with her the night she died, asleep in my room. I remembered nothing, I slept without incident, as far as I knew. The explosion alerted the neighbours to call the emergency services. I was still asleep when they arrived at the house. How on earth I slept through the explosion was a mystery to everyone. My room was completely undamaged. Amada mentioned to me a while back that she had been given a box containing some of my mother's personal things. It was time to ask Amada for the box.

I got up and went up to Amada's room. I knocked on her door.

"Come in." I entered and stood near the door.

"Hi honey. I will start dinner shortly; do you fancy anything in particular?" Amada was sitting in an armchair, with an open book facing downwards on her lap. The faint sound of a piano piece could be heard. "I could not sleep so decided to chillout with a book and Debussy."

"You do look more relaxed. Whatever you want to make for dinner is fine with me. Can I speak with you for a minute?"

"Yes, of course, come and sit." She waved her hand to the armchair opposite her." I entered the room fully and closed the door behind me. I took a seat. Amada observed me quietly, a gentle smile on her face. I took a deep breath and went straight for it.

"I would like to see the box of my mother's things, please." There was a flicker of surprise on Amada's face, followed by an understanding nod.

"I have been waiting and hoping that you would ask for the box. I must admit that I got worried as time passed, that you would not ask to see it. I intended to remind you that I still have it, after your exams." She got up and went into her walk-in wardrobe. She came out holding a box the size of a small packing box that was covered in a pink, purple and blue striped wrapping paper with a lid. A hazy memory came to mind – I wrapped the box and gave it to my mother with a birthday present inside. I made her a vase in my afterschool activity club. Amada held the box out to me.

"I have never opened it so can't tell you what is inside. I am glad you feel ready to go through the box. I am here if you need me." I took the box from her.

"Thanks. She has been popping into my head a lot recently." The box was not heavy. "Do you need any help with dinner?"

"I have it covered honey; dinner will be ready in about an hour. We are having spinach and pesto pasta, garlic bread and a green pine nut salad."

"Sounds good. I'll see you at dinner." I left with the box.

Now that I had the box, I was not ready to open it yet. I would wait until I had the house to myself. I didn't have any classes at college tomorrow. After my visit to the doctor. I will be the only one home until Grace gets home from school which would be around 4:10 PM at the earliest.

I placed the box at the back of my wardrobe and pulled my clothes forward to cover it. I felt restless, I needed to get out of the house. I pushed my phone into the back pocket of my jeans and took my purse out of my bag and headed downstairs. As I pulled on my coat, Amada came out of the kitchen.

"Hi honey, are you heading out?" There was worry in her eyes. I walked over to her and kissed her on the cheek.

"I just need some air. I may pop by and see Funmi. I'll see how I feel. Please don't hold dinner for me."

"Are you OK?"

"I haven't opened the box yet. I will open it tomorrow. I just need some air, see you later." I left before she could say another word. I had no specific destination in mind, I just walked.

Warning signals were going off in my mind. I was entering dangerous territories in my memory and the timing was bad. If I became unhinged, how would I study and pass my exams? The fort that kept the memories of my mother walled away in a dark corner of my mind was starting to crumble. I didn't know how to reinforce the walls.

The wind sent a blast of cold air into my face bringing my attention back to my surroundings. I realised that I was just yards from Calthorpe Park. I had just followed Pershore Road in the direction of the city centre. I turned onto Edward Road staying on the opposite side of the road from the park where there were houses. My sense of self-preservation made me weary of walking next to the park at night.

The street was quiet. There was no one else around, except for the person walking behind me. I frowned, realising that I had been hearing what sounded like the same footsteps behind, for some time. I stopped walking and turned round. The man behind me stopped walking too, stepping into the shadows. I continued walking, quickening my pace. I heard his footsteps behind me again matching my faster pace. Was he following me?

The hairs on the back of my neck stood up. I quickened my pace again and cast a quick look over my shoulder. He was still following me. I couldn't see his face; he was wearing a hoodie. He broke into a run towards me. I ran looking around frantically, hoping that if I screamed, I would be heard. I ran as fast as I could, glancing back to check how close he was behind me. I could ring the doorbell of one of the houses. But he could easily catch up with me before anyone answered the door. I cast another quick glance behind me. Panic was coursing through my veins. I ran smack into a wall of muscle. I screamed, terrified that he somehow got ahead of me. I fought frantically to break away from the hand holding my arm.

"Hey, calm down, are you OK?" The voice was commanding but conveyed concern. I took two steps back as my eyes focused on the wall of muscle I bumped into. The light was dim, I could not see his face clearly. It was a tall man dressed in jeans and a grey coat; it was not the man in the hoodie that had been following me. My eyes met the dark brown curious stare of the man I bumped into. I swung round my eyes searching for the man in the hoodie. He had vanished.

"Please help me, there was a man following me." I addressed the man I bumped into. My heart was pounding, adrenalin coursing through my veins. I bent and placed my hands on my knees letting my head hang forward whilst I caught my breath.

"Brissy, is that you?" I froze, how did he know my name? I straightened and backed away some more, my eyes fixed on his face. Squaring my shoulders, I stood tall.

"Who are you? How do you know my name?" He took a step towards me and raised his hands palms facing outwards.

"Please don't be afraid. I am Kade, Funmi's brother. We've met a handful of times." His deep voice was calm and reassuring. I studied his face, slowly my brain registered recognition, the panic ebbing away.

My eyes travelled to his; I traced the contours of his chiselled face. The cleanly shaven strong chin, the curve of his full lower lip topped by a defined 'M' shaped top lip. The thin line of a scar went from the corner of his top lip to his right ear. My eyes moved up to the well-shaped nose, past the commanding brown eyes to the black short, cropped hair on his head. I let out a deep sigh of relief.

"Hi, Kade, what a coincidence that you are my rescuer. I'm happy to see you. I was too freaked out to recognise you. Sorry." Kade's eyes flitted over my face.

"You said a man was following you, did you get a look at him, which direction did he go in?" I shook my head, still embracing the relief of being safe. Kade took out his phone, I frowned.

"You don't need to call Funmi, I am fine now. I couldn't see his face; he was wearing a hoodie."

"I'm not calling Funmi, I'm calling the police."

My eyes widened. "Why are you calling the police?"

Kade gave me a cool look. "Do you normally have an unknown man chasing you?"

Before I could respond he was speaking into the phone. "Hello, my name is Kade Diallo. An unknown man was following a lone female family friend on Edward Road." He paused listening. He continued to give an account of the situation. Followed by my full name and address as well as his own address and contact number. How did he even remember my full name and address?

"Yes, that's fine. We will come in to provide a full statement." He put his phone back in his pocket.

Kade turned his attention back to me; he studied me for a moment in silence. I shifted my weight from one foot to the other and gave him a nervous smile. The address he gave was right here on Edward Road. Not Funmi's home address. Funmi mentioned that he had a flat on Edward Road. He had clearly just left home as we were standing not far from his building.

"Why didn't you want to call the police? Don't you think you need to report what happened?" He watched my face intently. I cleared my throat.

"I suppose you're right. I' not thinking straight, I'm still a little freaked out."

"Where are you heading? Why are you out here alone?"

"I just needed some air; I came out for a walk. Thanks for your help, I'd better head home." Kade's eyes narrowed.

"Are you planning to walk home alone after what just happened?" I bit my lip.

"I feel perfectly safe now. I have never had any issues in the past in this area. I'm sure it was just a one-off incident. It's possible he was not following me, maybe I got my wires crossed." Even before I completed my last sentence, I didn't believe it. Whoever that man was, had been following me. That I was sure of.

"I could get a cab. But I'm sure I will be fine."

"Do you believe that you made a mistake, that he wasn't following you?" I was tempted to lie but the look in Kade's eyes told me he could already see the truth on my face.

"No. I'm sure he was following me."

"Thankfully, he did not harm you. But he could harm someone else. We need to go to the police station so you can provide a statement."

"What, now?"

"The sooner the better. My car is at the garage till tomorrow, I'll get us a cab." I didn't want to go to the police station. But Kade was right, what if the man attacked someone else? I would feel responsible. I watched him book the cab on his phone.

"It will be here in about five minutes." We stood in silence while waiting for the cab. Kade watched me openly. Thankfully, it did not take long before it arrived.

The cab pulled up next to us. The front passenger window rolled down. Kade leaned in and confirmed his details. He opened the back door and motioned for me to get in. I got in and slid to the other side of the seat. He got in after me.

We drove to the police station in silence save for the radio. The police station was only about ten minutes' drive into the city centre, assuming the traffic is light. I turned my face away from him and looked out of the window. I sensed an odd intent about my stalker. Who was he and what did he want from me?

"You look nervous. There is no need to be. Just tell the police what happened and answer their questions." I turned and gave Kade a brief smile.

"Being stalked is something that happens to other people, not little old me. I'm a little jittery."

"That's understandable."

"I can't stop outside the police station. I will drop you off at Colmore Row."

"That's fine, thanks." Kade responded to the cab driver. We got caught by the traffic lights. I watched the tram cross our path. Trams were still a relatively recent addition to Birmingham public transport. I keep meaning to take the trip to Wolverhampton in it but had not managed it yet. The driver pulled up in front of a supermarket on Colmore Row. We thanked him and got out. We made our way to the police station. We crossed the road and walked up the steps of the building. It had recently been refurbished and looked rather large and imposing. Kade paused before opening the door. He looked me in the eyes and gave a small smile.

"Brissy, relax, you haven't committed a crime. It will be fine; it should be a short process. Ready?" I took a deep breath and nodded giving him a grateful smile. We entered, Kade took my hand and we walked to the officer at the front desk. The warmth of his fingers gave me comfort. The officer looked up as we approached.

"Hello, how can I help you?" His calm assessing eyes glanced first at Kade then me.

"We're here to give a statement about the telephone report I made about twenty minutes ago.

The officer produced a clip board from behind the desk and cast his eyes over the paper on it. "Your name please."

"Kade Diallo and this is Brissy Jayne Yah." The officer nodded. He turned and called over one of his colleagues.

"Officer Mark Carson will take your statement, please follow him." Officer Carson gave us a friendly smile and led us to an interview room.

"Would you like a drink before we start?"

Kade shook his head, my throat felt very dry. "Some water would be great thanks." Kade walked over to the water fountain in the corner of the room and filled up a cup. He returned to the desk, placed the water next to my right hand and sat next to me.

"For the record, I am going to take your details again." After we provided our names, addresses, dates of birth and contact numbers, Officer Carson asked me what happened. I told him everything I remembered. He jotted down notes as I spoke and probed here and there with further questions When I was done, I felt a little silly. None of the information I provided could identify the man.

"That's it for now. If we need any further information or get a lead, we will be in touch."

When we walked out of the Police Station, I breathed a sigh of relief.

"Right, that was relatively painless. Have you had dinner?"

"Not yet."

"There's a particularly good little Chinese restaurant near my flat. I was heading there when our paths crossed. We can get a cab back, have dinner, then I'll walk you home. How about it?" Dinner with Kade – I was not sure it was a good idea. However, I was not ready to go home yet, and I could do with some food.

"OK, thanks." We walked back to Colmore Row and jumped in one of the taxis at the taxi rank. "When did you move into your flat and how are you settling in generally?" I wasn't sure what we would have to talk about over dinner. I guess I was about to find out.

"I moved in about a month ago, it's a nice little flat and I like the location. I can hop out of bed in the morning and go for a run in the park across the road. I have also been going for walks in Cannon Hill Park. It's great to have so much green space close by. I'm trying not to focus too much on how I'll adjust to civilian life in the long run. Just going with the flow for now. Some of the routine from the Army has stuck with me, but that's not such a bad thing."

"I love Cannon Hill Park, it's one of my favourite places in Birmingham." I twisted in my seat slightly towards him. It was a pleasant surprise to note that Kade appreciated open spaces.

"The restaurant is just ahead; please pull over here." Kade paid the driver and we got out. "Let's cross here." We crossed and turned into the small parking area in front of the restaurant. Kade held the door open for me to enter and followed me in." A woman with a warm smile came towards us.

"Kade, you are becoming a regular again. Who is your lovely friend?" I flicked a surprised look Kade's way.

"Hello Mui, you know I can't get enough of your special fried rice and ribs. This is Brissy, can we get a table please?"

He spoke to Mui with ease and familiarity. I gave her a little smile.

"There is a private table right in the corner, come with me." We followed Mui to a small table tucked away in the corner of the restaurant. I tried not to give too much thought to why Mui thought we should have a private table. The restaurant was busy for a Sunday evening, I guess the locals really like it. We hung our coats at the back of our chairs and sat down.

"Absolutely everything on the menu is good," said Kade. I had not eaten at the restaurant before; my local Chinese was a couple of minutes' walk from home. I scanned through the menu looking for their version of my usual. Salt and pepper chicken wings and chicken fried rice. It was a safe bet that they would have it, and they did. Mui returned to our table and we placed our order. Kade also ordered us stir fried vegetables, mini vegetarian spring rolls and a bottle of still water to share.

"I need to let Amada know where I am." I sent a quick message and included an apology for missing dinner. I placed my phone face down on the table.

"You are all grown up. I think it was about a year ago that I saw you last." There was a glint of amusement in his eyes. "I caught up with Funmi and Emmanuel this afternoon. They mentioned that they had lunch with you yesterday. Emmanuel seems to have developed a soft spot for you. Do you have a soft spot for my cousin too?" He watched me with a curious look in his eyes. I shifted in my seat, embarrassed at his words.

"Emmanuel is great company; I love his humour."

"Is that all you love about my cousin?" What was he getting at?

"We're just friends." I heard the familiar ping of a message. I picked up my phone and read Amada's simple response asking if I was OK. I sent her a reassurance and laid my phone down again.

"Amada got my message." Kade nodded.

"Tell me about your life, what's your plan after your A Levels?"

"I am hoping to do a Law and Business Studies degree at the University of Birmingham. I've been trying to schedule my time to get through all the studying and revision I have to do."

"Do you want to be a lawyer?"

"I'm not too sure. But I do have an interest in the legal system. What about you, what are your plans?" Our food arrived, Kade bit into a spring roll before responding.

"I'm still teasing out the details. Looking to open a self-defence centre. A close friend in the Army introduced me to martial arts four years ago. I've been immersed in martial arts since."

"Will your friend be partnering up with you in the new business?" Kade's fork paused halfway to his mouth. There was pain in his eyes as he looked at me. He cleared his throat and continued eating.

"I wish that were the case. Sadly, Bray died during an assignment to provide support to the Afghan security forces a year ago."

"I'm sorry Kade. I'm glad that you're home for good." We ate in silence for a few minutes.

"How is your food?" I smiled at him.

"It's so good."

"How are Amada, Grace and Marcus doing?"

"They're all good, thanks. You have a good memory for names." Again, I was surprised, he only met my family on a couple of occasions.

"Not particularly, perhaps I am making a special case for you." He watched me closely for a moment, my eyes widened. I stared at him dumbstruck. "What do you do with your free time?" I started to speak but my voice squeaked. I cleared my throat and tried again.

"I like walking, especially in Cannon Hill Park. Going out with friends, music, reading, theatre, the usual stuff."

"Are you wearing contact lenses? I remember your eyes being amber." He was looking directly into my eyes.

"You're right. My eyes were amber, now they are this colour, and no, I don't wear contact lenses." Perhaps it will simplify things if I just say I'm wearing contact lenses. He smiled.

"I sense a story there, but from your tone not one you want to get into now. That's fine, something to talk about another time. Do you want coffee?"

"Peppermint tea would be great, thanks." Mui appeared at our table as if by magic.

"How was your meal Brissy?" She asked smiling, her eyes full of curiosity.

"It was lovely thanks, as you can see I did it justice." I pointed at the empty dishes in front of me and smiled at her. She bowed her head slightly.

"Don't you want to know whether I enjoyed my food, Mui?" Kade asked in a teasing tone.

"You always enjoy your food, Kade. If you, didn't you would have told me already." Kade chuckled.

"Brissy would like a peppermint tea, and I will have my usual, thanks." Mui smiled and nodded. She stacked our dishes and took them away.

"How long have you been coming here?"

"Since I was about fifteen. I did delivery drops for Mui at the weekend for a year. Do you have classes at college tomorrow?" I gave him a cautious look.

"No classes tomorrow. I need to go out in the morning, then I'll be home for most of the day, studying."

"How about a walk in Cannon Hill Park, once you are done with your task in the morning?" He wanted to spend more time with me. I felt a fluttering sensation in my stomach. My dream came to mind. I said there was something between us, and that I wanted to explore it. Those words were true. I was attracted to Kade, but he was older. I don't have a lot of experience with the opposite sex. He was not like the boys I dated; he was a man. I needed to be cautious. There was an air of control about him. Something told me he could be ruthless if it suited him. But I did not feel threatened by him. Although he made me nervous.

"It's OK to say 'no', Brissy, if you would rather not go for a walk with me," Kade said softly. My eyes flickered up from the tablecloth that I had been staring at. His face and eyes gave no clue of what he was thinking.

"A walk would be nice. But I'm not sure what time I will be done at the doctors. Are you flexible on time?"

"Whatever time suits you is fine, I'm home all day tomorrow." Mui returned with our drinks and the bill. We sat in silence whilst we had our drinks.

"Ready?"

"Yes, thank you for the meal, it was lovely." Amusement flickered in his eyes.

"You are welcome, Brissy. Come on let's get you home." Kade paid for our meal, gave Mui a hug and we left. We walked along Pershore Road. It felt a little odd for us to be walking side by side but not touching. As if he read my mind, Kade took my left hand and placed it on his arm and shoved his hand into his coat pocket. I held his arm lightly with my gloved hand, it felt natural.

"You need some gloves."

"I keep forgetting to buy a pair, I will buy them tomorrow." An elderly couple were walking towards us. Kade steered me gently to make room for them to pass.

"Good evening," they both smiled as they greeted us.

Kade and I responded with a smile.

"They are lucky to have each other. Someone beside you to grow old together with is a gift. Perhaps that will be us one day." What the hell! Did Kade really see the two of us growing old together? I'd been doing my best to provide reasonable explanations that steered away from the obvious, despite the signals. The comment he just made demolished all my explanations and placed a spotlight on the obvious. I don't play games, I've no energy to invest in it. I want clarity; some straight talking was required after our walk tomorrow.

"Are you unwell, Brissy?" Kade's question took me off guard.

"No, why do you ask?"

"You said you were going to the doctor's tomorrow."

"Oh, it's because of the change in the colour of my eyes. My eye colour changed overnight; but I feel fine."

"That's odd, the colour is unusual too. Hopefully, it's nothing to worry about."

We walked on in silence. As we approached the Artful Dodger Pub; there was a commotion at the entrance. A group of young men came out. One of them stumbled into Kade separating us.

"Easy pal," Kade's tone was controlled. I moved to give the stumbling man room, so I was standing relatively close to the pub entrance. The guy regained his balance and apologised.

"Brissy Jayne Yah! My luck is in, glad I bumped into you." I turned, startled to hear my name. A young blond-haired man with tanned skin was standing by the pub door a huge grin on his face.

"Ben Collins, fancy seeing you here. When did you get back from Portugal?" Ben swept me up in his arms and twirled me around planting a kiss on my lips. His blue eyes were full of delight.

"I got back a couple of weeks ago. Planned to contact you to invite you to my birthday bash. How are the delightful Nikki, Funmi and Khadijah doing?"

"They're great." Ben had been living with relatives in Portugal for eight months teaching English. He looked happy and carefree.

"Ben! We need to go, cab's here." One of the young men that exited the pub yelled.

"Brissy, please come to my birthday bash. Nikki, Funmi and Khadijah are invited too. It would be great to catch-up", he reached for his mobile and sent a quick message, I heard my phone ping in receipt.

"I've sent you the details. I expect to see you there."

"I'll try and make it," I gave him a wide smile.

"Good, see you, Brissy." He gave me a quick hug and ran after his friends. I looked up and caught Kade's gaze. I walked over to him, hooked my arm through his and gently tugged on his arm to continue walking in the direction of my house.

"You seem pretty friendly with Ben."

"He's an old friend from my school days. We kept in touch. He's been living in Portugal teaching English. I envy him. I always hoped that I would be able to live and work abroad."

"What about your roots, have you ever been to Nigeria or Egypt?" Kade obviously gained quite a lot of information about me from Funmi.

"My mother used to tell me stories about her childhood days in Egypt. I know little about Nigeria; I haven't been to either country. But I hope to visit one day."

"I was born in Nigeria and lived there till I was ten. I have good memories of my childhood. There's a well-known family with your surname in northern Nigeria, not far from where my father's family live. They are from the same Fulani tribe as my father. Do you know much about your father's family?"

"No, my father died before I was born. My mother didn't know much about his family. She did say that his family background was Hausa-Fulani. I think there was some sort of family rift. When was the last time you went to Nigeria?"

"Eighteen months ago, for my father's funeral."

"Sorry, were you close to him?" Kade clearly had a lot to deal with recently. His father's death then his friend's death six months later.

"Yes, he was kind of a hero to me. He was a military man. I guess that is partly why I was drawn to joining the Army. I have four older half-brothers back in Nigeria, they all served in the military too. It was tough to leave them all when mum and I moved to the UK." We turned onto my road. I wished we had more time; I was riveted by Kade's history.

"You're home safe and sound, no more walks on your own at night please. What's your number?" I gave him my number, he dialled it when my phone rang, he cut the call. "Save my number. Let me know what time you want to meet for our walk tomorrow."

"Thanks for rescuing me and for dinner." I gave him a shy smile. We were standing outside my house.

"Good night, Brissy." Kade looked down at me. As he leaned down his eyes locked with mine. Our noses were almost touching. My heart was pounding in my ears. He brushed his lips against my cheek and straightened. There was a glint in his eyes – blast, he knew how I was feeling! I cleared my throat.

"Good night, Kade." I walked to my front door, let myself in and shut the door without looking back. I leaned against the door, willing my racing heart to slow down.

ೞೞೞ

8. REVELATIONS

There was laughter coming from the living room and I could hear the TV. I went to the door and popped my head in. Amada and Grace were sitting on the sofa.

"Brissy, come and join us, this show is hilarious," said Grace.

"Hi, I am going to put in a couple of hours of study then go to bed."

"How was dinner with Kade, and how is he finding civilian life?" Amada watched me carefully as she spoke.

"Dinner was lovely, thanks, Kade is good. I'll see you both in the morning."

"I will pop in to say good night," said Amada.

"Good night, Brissy. You can tell me how you got on with gorgeous Kade tomorrow," said Grace. There was a mischievous look on her face. I looked at her with a raised eyebrow and left.

I stopped by the bathroom, washed my face, and brushed my teeth and went into my room. I stripped off my clothes, put on my PJs and sat at my desk. My evening had been interesting to say the least. Now I needed to focus my attention on my work for the next couple of hours. I picked up the book for my English Literature assignment paper and started reading. I made notes as I read.

I was startled by a hand on my shoulder.

"Sorry I startled you, honey. I knocked but you did not hear me. That book must be riveting." I smiled.

"It is a good story, quite sad in places. I have to write a critical assessment of it for my English Literature assignment paper."

"I just came to see how you are doing and say good night." Her probing eyes scrutinised my face.

"I did get a little upset about my mother after I took the box from you, and I do feel anxious about opening it. I was planning to open it tomorrow when I had the house to myself. But now, I really don't know."

"If you would like, I can sit quietly in the room with you while you open it. You don't have to say anything to me about what is in the box. I can come home at 3pm tomorrow so you can open it while the house is quiet. Alternatively, you can open it on Tuesday morning, I won't be going to work till around midday."

"Thanks, I would like that. Tuesday morning sounds good." I stood up and gave her a hug. She kissed me on the cheek.

"Good night, honey."

"Good night." I watched her quietly leave my room. I felt better about opening the box. I stretched; I was ready for bed. I saved Kade's number and read Ben's message, his birthday party is next Saturday evening. I forwarded the message to Nikki, Funmi and Khadijah with details of my encounter with Ben.

I got into bed. I wondered what Kade was doing right now. The little butterflies returned to my stomach. I curbed the temptation to start dissecting the time I spent with him. I would have a frank conversation with him tomorrow as to what he wanted from me, friendship, or something more. I sighed and closed my eyes. An image of the hooded man popped into my head. Who was my stalker and what did he want? For once, I wished away my hours of slumber as I closed my eyes.

"Hello Brissy, I have been waiting for you." I was back in the dream world, on the path. Soraya was sitting on one of the benches.

"Hello Soraya, it does seem like a long time since our last encounter. I have a lot of questions for you. Some very strange and scary things have been happening to me." Soraya nodded, I sat down next to her.

"I am aware of the things you have been experiencing."

"You know?"

"Yes, I know. You are a Gene Bearer, a Mutata."

"What's that?"

"You have a gene mutation - the Chrysalis Gene mutation. Less than 1% of the world's population have the gene mutation. In about 5% of the Gene Bearer population the gene is activated. Those with the activated gene are the Mutata. The Gene Bearers with the dormant gene are known as Echoers."

"You are saying I am some sort of mutant – that explains a lot!" Soraya smiled.

"I would not put it like that. Let's just say you are a rarity."

"That is a rosy way of seeing it. What I hear is, you are confirming what I always suspected. I am a freak!"

"No Brissy, you are unique. Being a Mutata gives you an immeasurable opportunity to do good. Embrace your capabilities and choose to use it to help those around you. There are a lot of challenges ahead of you, but so much potential for you to help and influence the lives of all sorts of people for the better. Many wish they can make an actual difference to the world; few will ever really have that ability. You can make a difference." I didn't want to be a saviour to anyone. I just wanted to be a normal teenager and experience the world in a normal way – whatever that meant.

"Hold on a second. How do you know all this stuff about the Chrysalis Gene? You say you are part of my mind, but how can you have all this information, when I don't?"

"The Mutata are able to access a special wave energy frequency called the Cognition Cascade Link, or CC Link. The link allows the Mutata to share information. Think of it like uploading and downloading an encrypted computer file. I am the password that gives your mind access. The information is not neatly categorised, it's more like a data dump."

"So, all Mutata have someone like you to guide them?"

"Yes. We are referred to as Guardians. The connection between the Mutata and Guardian varies considerably. The closer the connection the greater the capabilities. Guardians mirror the capabilities of the Mutata."

"What am I in for?" A heavy feeling settled in my stomach.

"The Chrysalis Gene primarily controls brain function. It can enhance the performance of every part of the brain to unknown levels. The things that are common to all Mutata is that they can hear and control the minds of others. They have an incredible intuition. There is even a record of one individual who appeared to be able to see the future. The Mutata can hear most thoughts, and sense, most feelings being experienced by those around them. But they can't hear the thoughts or feel the emotions of other Gene Bearers. Beyond that, the capability of each Mutata differs considerably."

Soraya watched me in silence for a few minutes. I looked off into the distance following the white path as far as I could see.

"What now? I don't know what to do with what you just told me."

"An organisation called Pro-Tego monitors and provides support to all Gene Bearers. Pro-Tego allocates a type of coach to all Gene Bearers. They are called Overseers. An Overseer sometimes looks after multiple Gene Bearers. Martha Maddison is the Overseer allocated to you, Kade and Marcus." I listened intently. Distancing myself from the pangs of dread I felt.

"What do Kade, and Marcus have to do with all this?"

"Kade and Marcus are Echoers." It keeps getting better!

"You have to contact Martha; she will fill you in on the rest of what you need to know. I still have a lot to learn about the Chrysalis Gene. The information in the CC Link is vast. Finding and assimilating key information is going to be an ongoing process."

"What do you know about the man who was following me? Something tells me he had a specific purpose beyond the usual criminality." Soraya nodded, a pleased look on her face.

"Good, your intuition is gaining strength. You are right. The man that followed you was sent by a rogue organisation called Zraykus. They believe Gene Bearers are defective, a mistake of nature and a threat to the rest of humanity. Given the opportunity they will harm, even kill a Gene Bearer. The man's goal was to mute your ability to transmit frequencies. This technique uses a modified artificial wave energy frequency emitted by an electrical device. It works on about half of the Mutata, it can kill. I detected his purpose and was able to bolster your gene defence. He was unsuccessful from a distance, so he was trying to get closer to you. Kade's presence assisted, I tapped into his echo frequency to increase your defence. His proximity to you at the time of the attempted attack was key to my success. Zraykus have lost their window of opportunity to stop the development of your capabilities. But they will work against you in other ways, you need to be on your guard."

I could feel a familiar pressure in my head. Was it possible to get a migraine in one's sleep? I don't want to hear any more, what I heard was pretty indigestible.

"Look, I need time to digest this crazy stuff. I don't want to contact Martha yet, I want time to think."

"Time is not on your side. The pace of your transformation will increase with every passing day. You can't delay contacting Martha." My hands curled into fists.

"What the hell am I transforming into exactly? Do you know?" Soraya's eyes were full of empathy as she shook her head.

"I don't know, it remains to be seen."

"Right, in that case, I am taking a couple of days to digest this stuff. Then I'll contact Martha."

"Very well. I know this is a lot to get your head around. Remember that you are not alone, you have me. Once Kade and Marcus speak to Martha, you will be able to share the experience with them as well. You will be able to support each other. Visit your doctor tomorrow, it is important that you go. When you see the doctor, I want you to make a cerebral connection, and send thoughts to his mind that you are fine and there is nothing to be concerned about. You have gained access to sufficient wave energy to influence the minds of those around you in a controlled way if you concentrate. It is important that you remember that you must not tell the doctor about your capabilities. Also, you must not allow a scan to be taken of your brain. A scan will reveal the unusual level of activity going on in your brain. I can only communicate with you at present while you are asleep. That will change as your capabilities grow."

"My life as I envisaged it, all my goals and hopes have just been smashed. My life agenda is no longer mine to control. The Chrysalis Gene now has control." I made the statement as a neutral recognition of my new normal. Soraya leaned towards me.

"You have always been this person, Brissy, you just did not know it. You cannot go back to who you thought you were. You can only move forward in full knowledge of who you are. Your new path will become clearer to you as the days go by. Please engage with Martha, she is there to assist you. She will also offer support to Kade and Marcus, they will be told of their status. We are out of time; I will see you in your sleep tonight."

I heard the intrusive sound of my alarm going off and was dragged back into consciousness. I did not linger in bed, I got up, showered and dressed. At 8:00 AM sharp I called the doctor's surgery and made an appointment for 10:00 AM.

I dislike visiting doctors, hospitals, and dentists. Opticians were the only ones I could tolerate. Amada and I were sitting in the waiting room of the doctor's surgery. I could hear the faint hum of the minds of other patients. The experience was weird to say the least. I listened to the varied thoughts of my fellow patients. There was nothing extraordinary save for one mind.

A woman in her twenties in the opposite row of chairs, was sitting in a defeated stoop, her head hung. She had a small frame that was clearly too thin. The words "I want to die echoed over and over in her mind. A chill ran through me. She intended to take her own life tonight. The compulsion to make a cerebral connection with her mind was almost overwhelming. But what if I screwed it up? I might fry her brain! I didn't want to grant her wish to die. I took a deep breath. If I can help her in some way, it was worth the risk. My hands trembled, I clenched them into fists on my lap. I focused my mind on hers and made a cerebral connection.

The air felt strange, like it was charged with electricity. I bowed my head continuing to focus on maintaining my connection to her. Beads of sweat broke out on my forehead; I felt hot then cold. I raised my head and looked at her. My gasp was audible. My nervous gaze flitted to Amada then around the waiting room. Thankfully, no one was paying any attention to me. My eyes fixed on the area just above her head. I wanted to take a closer look at the blue aura. It started to fade as my connection weakened.

Focus – I closed my eyes and focused all my energy on her. I am not sure what I was expecting but it was not this. It was like watching clips of a disjointed film. My eyes opened and settled on her. She lost a child in the last year or so and the pain was so raw it brought tears to my eyes. She was broken in every sense; she could no longer bear her sorrow. My heart went out to her. She lifted her head and looked straight at me.

It was clear that she didn't really see me, her eyes were empty. Mirroring the crater of emptiness that existed in her soul. Well, not quite empty, there was a dim flame of feelings still present within her. The flame was for someone called Sam. I glanced at the man sitting next to her. Sam.

His face was drawn, his worried eyes darted across the woman's face – Anna, her name is Anna.

I had a flash of an image of Anna holding a baby girl. Sam stood close, his arms around Anna's shoulder as he gazed at his daughter. I was certain it was the future not the past that I had just seen. I gripped the arm of my chair; something had changed again. I just had a premonition, while awake! Anna would be a mother again if she could be motivated to live. Anna needed to get a glimpse of the wonderful future that awaited her and Sam.

I focused all my energy on both Anna and Sam. If I could share the images of their daughter with them at the same time. It would carry more weight if they both had the same vision and knew that they shared the vision. I took three deep silent breaths and focused on Anna and Sam. Maintaining my cerebral connection to Anna whilst connecting to Sam's mind.

A gasp came from Anna. She clasped her hands over her mouth eyes wide. She turned to Sam. He looked like he had been hit in the gut. Tears started rolling down Anna's cheeks.

"Sam, did you see her? Did you see our baby girl?" Sam turned to Anna still in shock. Nodding, he quickly wiped away tears. He tried to speak but no words came out. He cleared his throat.

"I saw her, Anna, our baby girl, I saw her." Sam reached for Anna and they held on to each other. Anna's body shook as she sobbed, tears of relief, gratitude and hope washed away much of the sorrow. Anna spoke through her tears.

"Let's go home, Sam." Sam nodded his agreement, and they left the surgery arms around each other's waist. I glanced around the waiting room, thankful other patients were in another section of the long room, they hadn't noticed anything out of the ordinary. Amada was scrolling through messages on her phone, she glanced up.

"Brissy honey, are you OK?" Amada was looking at me with concern. "Why are you crying? What's wrong?" I hadn't noticed that tears were running down my face. I was absorbing some of Anna and Sam's feelings.

"I am fine, Amada, in fact I am great, I had a wonderful thought." I leaned closer to her, "I think I am a bit emotional, it's that time of the month." Amada took the bait. She smiled and gave me some tissue to mop up my face. My mother's words came back to me. She said I would help make the lives of other people better. It's a wonderful feeling. I was sure that Anna no longer wanted to take her own life, and that she would overcome her struggles. Be happy again.

My name was announced, I was required to go to Room 4 to see Dr Johnson. Amada and I went to Dr Johnson's consultation room. I knocked on the door and was invited to enter.

"Good morning, is it Brissy?"

"Yes, morning. This is my foster mum." Dr Johnson is a middle-aged man with gentle eyes. He gestured that we should take a seat.

"What can I do for you today, Brissy?" I really hoped I could pull off making another cerebral connection. I had to make Dr Johnson believe that there was nothing to be concerned about – no tests were needed.

"Last night I had a distressing dream; I don't remember the details." I was fibbing. "I woke up with …" I hesitated, "a change in my eye colour and was very tired." I knew that if I did not provide sufficient details to Dr Johnson, Amada would happily fill in the blanks.

"What is the usual colour of your eyes Brissy?"

"Amber." I was struggling to respond to questions, maintain a cerebral connection and focus on influencing his thoughts.

"That is a material change in colour. Has there been any change in your vision? Headaches, loss of appetite, weight gain or loss?"

"No, other than feeling very tired yesterday when I woke up; I feel fine. My energy levels are almost normal again, I'm fine." I tried to affirm my confirmation that I am fine by sending the same thoughts to Dr Johnson. He examined my eyes, shining a light into them.

"It is not unheard of for adult eye colour to lighten or darken. But it occurs in a small minority of the elderly. You seem to be generally well and healthy. No major alarm bells are ringing. I could send you for a CT scan. But I think we may be jumping the gun to do that now. My recommendation is that you make an appointment to see your optician. They can do a more detailed examination of your eyes. If you get the all clear, we do not need to do anything else. If there is an issue, you need to come back and see me.

I gave an inward sigh of relief at Dr Johnson's assessment and recommendation. I hoped Amada would not insist that I get the CT scan.

"Thank you, Dr Johnson. I'll make an appointment and see my optician. I'll come and see you if there's any further concerns. Have a good day," I quickly ended the conversation. Gave Dr Johnson a bright smile and took Amada's arm leading her firmly out of the room.

Phew, it had gone well. I knew that Dr Johnson received my message that I was fine, but I had no idea whether it influenced his recommendations. As we left the Surgery, I gave Amada a reassuring smile.

"I'll make an appointment to see the optician. I am fine, and I am sure I will be given the all clear." Amada accepted my reassurance.

"I want you to stay home for the next couple of days and rest. Regain your strength fully before you return to college. You can go back to college on Wednesday and hopefully you can see the optician on Wednesday too."

"Agreed. Please don't worry about me." Amada shook her head.

"I feel good and optimistic right now."

"Enjoy your good mood and state of mind. Draw on it when you open the box. I am going to head to work now, I will see you at home this evening." I gave her a hug and waved her off.

9. NEW NORMAL

I made my way to Cannon Hill Park. I still felt an unnatural degree of calm bearing in mind all that Soraya told me. Hearing the thoughts of others was beginning to feel normal too. I could dial my attention up or down as I pleased. I was relieved when Soraya informed me that I couldn't hear the thoughts of other Gene Bearers. That meant that I couldn't hear Kade's thoughts. I preferred to allow our relationship to unfold as naturally as possible.

I paused outside the entrance to the MAC. Sent Kade a text that I was in the MAC. Hopefully, he would not take too long to arrive. In the meanwhile, I was looking forward to checking out the exhibitions inside the MAC. I had a spring in my step as I entered.

It was busy downstairs as usual. It usually was, because of the restaurant and bar areas. I went straight upstairs heading for the tapestry displays. I was engrossed in the beautiful rich display of colourful creations, when I felt arms go around my waist from behind and pull me into a muscular form behind me. It was Kade. I knew it without turning around.

"Do you see anything you like?" He spoke into my ear, his warm breath fanning my cheeks. How on earth had he got here so quickly? I was tempted to turn around but was afraid it would be harder to be so close to him and look him in the eye.

"This piece is rather lovely, don't you think?" My voice was surprisingly even given the turmoil I felt. I hoped he would not ask me what I liked about the tapestry because I would struggle to string my sentences together. I willed myself to be calm.

"Exquisite, I think it's one of a kind. The piece attracts so much attention, yet it is oblivious to its rare beauty." His words made me smile.

"I didn't know you had such a creative eye."

"Let's just say, I keep surprising myself when it comes to this rare find."

I cleared my throat. "Hello Kade. How did you get here so quickly?"

"I've been here for the last hour or so, reading and people watching." I turned round slowly. He kept his arms around me foiling my attempt to put some distance between us. His warm brown gaze searched my face, his eyes returned to mine. We stood there looking into each other's eyes. He bent his head and softly brushed his lips against mine. I lowered my eyelids and stopped breathing. When he lifted his head there was a serious look on his face.

"I missed you all night. When I woke up this morning, you were still on my mind. Until last night I hadn't seen you in almost a year. Yet having you close to me feels like the most natural thing in the world." I needed fresh air; this was all getting too much to handle. I reached behind me and parted his hands breaking his embrace. Holding one of his hands, I tugged him in the direction of the stairs.

"I think we should go for that walk now."

"Hello, lassie, I have not seen you around here for a little while." I turned in the direction of the voice. My face lit up.

"Max! How lovely to see you, when did you return to work?" I pulled Kade along with me, until we reached Max. Max is an elderly security man. He had worked at the MAC for at least as long as I'd been coming here. He'd been off work, ill, for several weeks. It was great to see him looking well again. "I missed you, you look well. How are you feeling?"

"As good as new lassie! It's a treat to see your lovely face again. I missed your wonderful smile." He gave me a solemn look. "It saddens me that I was right. The new colour of your eyes confirms my suspicion. You are one of the fay folks." I burst out laughing.

"Oh Max, you and your legends and fairy tales," I gave him an indulgent smile.

"Are you going to introduce me to your young man?"

"Max meet Kade, Kade meet one of my favourite people – Max." Max beamed at me, then looked at Kade.

"You are a lucky lad, Kade. Brissy here is a rare gem, look after her." Kade stepped forward smiling and held out his hand to Max.

"Nice to meet you Max." They shook hands. "I know a rare gem when I see one. I have found a treasure that I intend to hold on to. I will treat her with great care." Max nodded in approval.

"You are a wise man, Kade."

"Right gentlemen. This treasure would like to go for a walk and get some fresh air. Max, I am glad you're back. The place is not the same without you. I'll be seeing you." I gave him a small salute; he smiled and returned my salute.

"See you, lassie, nice to meet you Kade."

"Likewise, Max." I gave Max a final wave and went down the stairs and out of the doors into the park. Kade was right behind me. I buttoned up my coat, pulled my hood over my head and pulled on my gloves. "Do you have a preferred route?" Kade put on his coat and turned up the collar. I noticed for the first time that he was wearing black jeans and a black polo neck, the strength of his muscular body still visible beneath his grey coat.

"People are drawn to you, have you noticed that?"

I looked at him in surprise. "Are they? If you are referring to Max, I have known him since I was twelve years old. I met him on the first day of my visit to the MAC, he is a sweetie."

"Not just Max. I reached my conclusion based on my observations over the years. I usually walk towards the boating lake. On your last visit to the park, you and Amada walked away from it. I think we should both take a different route. How about we take the path ahead of us?"

"Sure. You saw me and Amada yesterday?"

"I did. It didn't seem like a good time to say hello." He took my hand and placed it on his arm and put his hand in his pocket. Just like last night. We walked in silence for about five minutes.

"Are you seeing anyone?" The question caught me off guard, I turned to look at him briefly then looked ahead again.

"No, why?"

"Because…I would like to find out what's between us. My intention had been to stay away from you. You are young, possibly too young for me. But fate keeps putting you in my path, and there is the fact that I keep thinking about you." This was the reverse of my dream; I didn't have to persuade him to see where things took us. He was offering me what I wanted in my dream. Soraya said that I could not hear his mind – that was true. I don't think I can influence his mind using my capabilities either. I'll check with her just to be sure. This request appeared to be of his own free will.

"You want us to date?"

"I want a little more than that, Brissy. I want exclusivity, no games. I want to find out what kind of a relationship we could have. I am not looking to rush you into anything. I am happy to take things slow. I want us to be a couple whilst we explore what we can be to each other." He looked straight ahead, he hadn't looked at me once. Now he stopped walking and turned me to face him. I was still digesting his words. Kade wanted us to be a couple. It felt like I was dreaming. He looked at me patiently waiting for my response.

"I'm not sure what to say, Kade." His expression gave nothing away.

"Then you should give it some thought before you give me your response. I can wait, we have time." I did want some time to think this through and I wanted to know that I was not influencing his mind. We continued walking; I took his arm again.

"Just to be clear, Kade, I am very attracted to you, I think you know that."

"It's good to know that my naked body left a lasting impression on you." He said softly, casting a sideways look at me. My face felt ridiculously hot, despite the cold.

"That was a …memorable day. But I don't just want your body. Going into a serious relationship with you would be a big deal for me. I haven't had that much experience with men." Kade suddenly stopped walking. He turned me to face him again. A surprised look on his face.

"Brissy, are you a virgin?" My face was beyond hot now; it felt like the top of my head just burst into flames. The look on my face must have been quite a picture.

"Well, that is a surprise. I wasn't expecting that. We would have to take it slow for sure. I'm not looking for you to jump into bed with me." I felt embarrassed, immature, and very inexperienced. Somewhat annoyed too. Though I'm not sure exactly why I was annoyed. My eyes narrowed, and I moved closer to Kade. Holding his gaze, I wound my arms around his neck and pressed my body to his.

"What if I wanted to jump your bones, Kade, would you still want to take it slow?" His eyes were full of intrigue. "Let's do a little test run." I pulled his head down and kissed him deeply. His hand went around my waist and pulled me tightly to him, he kissed me back. I felt a deep hunger and I fed it. Our mouths finally broke apart for air, we were both breathing heavily. I wriggled against Kade intending to break free from him. He groaned; his face buried in my neck.

"Please don't do that, just be still for a minute." I was about to ask why but froze instead. I complied and stood perfectly still. I was thankful he couldn't see my face. He released me and took a step back from me. Desire still lingered in his eyes as he looked at me.

"Your little test run got more of a reaction than you bargained for. It's been a while. You may be a virgin but you sure as hell don't kiss like one!" I looked down shifting my weight from one foot to the other.

"Sorry. I guess I was trying to prove a point. It took me by surprise too."

Kade laughed. "In response to your question, you are welcome to jump my bones any time you want." He held out his arms wide and waggled his eyebrows suggestively. I couldn't help laughing too. He took my hand and we continued walking.

"What did the doctor say about the change in your eye colour?"

"He said it was unusual. But he wasn't too concerned as I am not experiencing any problems. He just asked me to go and see my optician to get a full eye examination. If any issues are found, I have to go back and see him."

"Good. Sure, you are feeling, OK?"

"Yes, absolutely fine. I could do with some food though; I am pretty hungry."

"Me too. We can either eat at the MAC or we can go into the city centre for more choice.

"Let's head into town."

"My car is in the carpark." We turned around retracing our steps. My back stiffened. I could feel a strong tingling sensation, in my fingertips; something was wrong. I cast my eyes around. My gaze settled on three teenagers who looked like they should be in school. Two of them had Staffordshire Bull Terriers on a leash. The dogs were barking aggressively and growling. One of them tugged on the leash, the boy holding it lost his grip. The dog ran towards a group of children. I tugged my hand free from Kade and ran towards the children, the dog was closing in. Barking and growling. The women suddenly realised the danger and screamed running to grab the children. I took the scarf from around my neck and wrapped it around my left hand and forearm. I heard Kade shouting my name and running after me.

The dog lunged at one of the children. One of the women placed herself between the dog and the child. It locked its teeth on her calf tugging. She screamed. The children were being rushed to safety. I grabbed the dog's back legs and lifted it high off the ground. It let go of the woman's calf and I quickly let go of its legs as it turned on me. I offered up my protected hand; it bit into it hard.

I made a cerebral connection and commanded the dog to stop. Nothing. It continued to bite into my scarf, and hand beneath. I could now feel its teeth in my flesh.

"Stop," I shouted. It immediately let go of my hand and stood there looking at me. "Sit," I commanded, it sat. All the aggression left it. Kade was now by my side. I wanted to be sure that the dog would not attack again. "Stay," the dog lay flat on its belly and placed its large head between its front legs, its eyes fixed on me. It whimpered quietly. Kade pulled me away from where the dog lay.

"Let me see your hand." He started unravelling my scarf from my injured hand.

"It's not that bad, I am OK. Help the lady, he bit her pretty hard." Kade checked on the woman. She was in shock. A man stepped forward from the crowd. He said the police and an ambulance were on their way. He took the woman's hands and spoke to her softly telling her she was going to be fine, that help was on its way. Kade took off his scarf and tied it tightly around the woman's bleeding calf. He returned to my side. He removed my scarf from my hand and looked at the damage.

The boy who owned the dog broke through the crowd. He picked up the dog's leash and tugged on it.

"Come on boy, let's go." The dog whimpered but did not move. The boy cast me an evil look.

"You bitch! What did you do to my dog?" Kade stepped in.

"Shut the hell up!" His voice was thick with anger. "You stay right there with your dog. You can explain to the police, why your dog was so aggressive and attacked unprovoked."

"I'm not hanging about; I am out of here." Kade stiffened, about to take a step towards the boy. I placed my uninjured hand on his arm.

"His not going anywhere. He knows the right thing is to wait for the police, so that's what he is going to do." My mind issued the same command to the dog owner – stay. The boy sat down next to his dog.

"You scared the crap out of me, Brissy. The dog could have really hurt you." He examined my injured hand again. "All things considered, you got off lightly." He looked at the four puncture marks on my hand. No bones were broken. He was right, I was lucky. I glanced at the dog; it was still lying motionless on the ground looking at me.

"Thank you so much, I don't know how you got the dog to listen to you. It is nothing short of a miracle. It could have been terrible but for you." Said the woman who the dog bit on the calf. I nodded and smiled at her.

"I'm glad that everyone is going to be OK."

The police arrived. The boy was handed a muzzle and told to put it on his dog. I made eye contact with the dog. I felt sorry for the poor thing, it was still unclear why it attacked. It would almost certainly be destroyed. It could no longer be trusted to be in a public space. The boy may have some answers. I focused on his mind, searching for a reason for the dog's behaviour. I saw images of a dog fight, the baits used looked like dolls. That explained why the dog went for the children. I took a deep breath, angry at the boy and sad for the dog.

I transmitted instructions requiring the boy to tell the police what he had been doing to the poor dog. As soon as the officer asked about the dog's behaviour, he would offer up the information. One of the officers picked up the dog's leash and tried to pull the dog up. I instructed the dog to get up, stay calm and go with the officer.

The officer led the dog away. Another officer was taking statements, I gave him my account.

"Officer, you should ask the boy about the dog's behaviour. Something must have made him attack. Do you have any more questions for us?"

"Not right now, you are free to go, Miss. Please go to the hospital to get your hand seen to. You may need a shot for the bite. You did a heroic thing today, take care of yourself."

"Thank you." Kade was already by my side, he placed his arm around my waist and steered me towards the exit to the car park.

ಬಿ‌ಇ‌ಬಿ

10. WHAT, WHEN, HOW

Two and a half hours later we were leaving the QE Hospital's A&E Department heading for Kade's car. A nurse cleaned and dressed my injured hand and gave me a tetanus jab. Kade quietly sat with me, his eyes full of questions he was deferring for now. He asked whether I wanted him to call my family. I'd declined, my hand was not severely injured, I was fine. We got into the car, Kade turned in his seat to look at me.

"We need to talk. Can you come to my flat?" His eyes were neutral, even though I could not hear his thoughts, I did not need to. I knew exactly what he wanted to talk about. I could fob him off and delay the inevitable for a while. It would be difficult to tell the truth without a full explanation, but that's what I would have to do for now. He would be given the full facts soon enough.

"Sure, if you promise to feed me." My stomach was reminding me that lunch was overdue. He turned back to face the steering wheel, put on his seat belt, and started the car.

"If you feel up to it, we can stop by the supermarket on the way. If not, I can drop you off at my flat and come back out to pick up some food."

"I'm fine, let's pick up some shopping." I turned on the radio. Rested my head against the back of the seat and looked out of the window. I would have to contact Martha tomorrow. It was beginning to feel like timelines were speeding up. I need help.

I also need to call Funmi. I would have to give her a detailed account of what was going on between Kade and me. I believed she would be supportive but hoped she would not probe too deeply. Kade pulled into the car park of a supermarket close to his flat.

"Come on. Let's pick up what we need for lunch. I also need some essentials, there's not much in my fridge and cupboards." I got out of the car and followed him into the supermarket. He took one of the trollies near the entrance.

"Let's get the essentials first then we can visit the Deli and bakery." We whizzed through the aisles. Kade picked up items from the shelves putting them in the trolley. He paused at the fruit section.

"What fruits do you like?"

"I eat most fruits. The apples and yellow plums look good." He added them to the growing heap in the trolley. "We need butter for the French loaf. I love crusty bread and butter; I could make a meal of it. Here we go - butter, and some cheese too." I wandered over to the display of chocolates on the opposite aisle and picked up a pack of my favourite milk chocolates. Kade came up behind me.

"Sweet tooth?" I nodded.

"It runs away with me sometimes. Don't let me eat too many in one go!"

"Judging from the speed with which you took off in the park, there's no need to be concerned about your fitness levels. You were extremely fast!" I looked down and steered him and the trolley towards the Deli. Kade had a point. I had been quick; energy simply coursed through me. Soraya did not said anything about super speed. I took a silent deep breath. I would cope with whatever there was to come. I had to cope. The knot of hunger in my stomach brought my attention back to what I wanted for lunch.

"I fancy garlic and herb roast chicken; they do a nice coleslaw and I think some olives to go on the side with the mixed salad leaves. I will take a couple of slices of the French loaf. You can munch the rest with butter to your heart's content." I gave him a bright smile.

"I get the message, our talk can wait, but we are going to talk." He gave me a steady look. "I'm glad you have a good appetite. Let's go get the rest of the items for our lunch plate." We quickly picked up the items for lunch. Kade paid and we exited the supermarket with the trolley filled with a generous number of shopping bags.

"Kade, darling." We both turned towards the husky female voice. I recognised her immediately as the girl with Kade at Funmi's sixteenth birthday party. She walked towards us hips swinging. She was dressed in black skinny jeans, three-inch heel boots and a black suede coat. Her long red hair cascaded down her back. She looked stunning. It struck me that we could not be more different in looks. Other than the fact that we are both tall, there is zero similarity in our looks. Kade smiled at her.

"Hello Clarice, this is a surprise. How are you?" Kade's tone was casual.

"Don't be so formal, darling." Clarice wound her arms around Kade's neck, pressed her body to his and kissed him on the lips. Kade unclasped her arms from around his neck and took a step back. Clarice's eyes narrowed as she looked at Kade. Her gaze then moved to me. Her eyes were cold and dismissive. She turned her attention back to Kade.

"Aren't you going to introduce me to your friend?" Her tone was mocking, Kade's jaw tightened.

"Brissy meet Clarice, Clarice meet Brissy." Clarice turned to me again, giving me her full attention this time. A scowl settled on her face.

"Have we met before?"

"Possibly at Funmi's sixteenth birthday party, I think you were there that night." I said with a smile. Something flashed in Clarice's eyes. Her lips tightened.

"Yes, I remember you now." She glanced from me to the shopping trolley and back to Kade. Waving her hand at the shopping she said, "all this looks terribly domesticated. What's going on?"

"What are you doing in Birmingham, I thought you were still in New York?" Kade's tone was dry and disinterested.

"I was offered a one-year contract with a cosmetics company. I thought it might be good to return home for a bit." My heart sank. Clarice would be around for a whole year. "How long is your leave?" "It would be nice to catch-up."

"I have left the Army; I'm home for good."

"That's great news, fate is on our side. We can take walks down memory lane." She gave Kade a knowing look. "You remember how good we were together, don't you, Kade?" Kade's face remained expressionless.

"That was in the past Clarice. I'm not free to take a trip down memory lane with you. Our past will be staying in the past."

Her eyes widened; she threw a brief scornful look in my direction.

"Kade, she's a baby. When did you start picking up schoolgirls?" She spoke about me as if I were a dim-witted child who could not understand the conversation. My anger rose, as I heard the hateful thoughts going through her mind. I immediately quenched it.

"Good luck with your new assignment. Excuse us." Kade took my elbow with one hand and steered the trolley with the other hand.

"I'll be seeing you Kade." He kept on walking and did not respond. I could feel her eyes on us as we headed for the car.

"What a bitch! Something tells me that's not the last we've heard from Clarice." My tone was dry. Kade cast a sideways glance at me.

"I am sorry about Clarice; she's used to getting what she wants. People don't normally say 'no' to her."

"She still considers you hers. Judging from her performance just now, she won't let you go without a fight." The idea of getting into a battle with Clarice didn't fill me with joy. But fight I would if I had to. The thought made me pause. It looks like I've made my decision about Kade's invitation to start a relationship with him. Clarice would not fight fair. It's the last thing I need right now. My plate was being heaped with challenge after challenge. I too sighed. I gave Kade a tired smile.

"Don't worry about Clarice, I can handle her. Take a seat in the car. I'll put the shopping in the boot and join you after I put the trolley back." I got in the car, grateful for a few minutes to myself. My hand was throbbing. Leaning my head back against the seat I closed my eyes.

"You can use your willpower to take away the pain." My eyes flew open as Soraya's words came into my mind.

"Soraya, I am awake! How are you communicating with me?"

"I thought it would take longer before I could communicate with your conscious mind. But the progress of your transformation is following an unusually expedited pattern. Will the pain away Brissy, it is within your capability." I closed my eyes again and looked forward to a point when I was free of pain, with my wounds healing. My eyes opened wide.

"Goodness, it worked! I also saw my hand healing."

"That is impressive, your wounds have healed by about twenty percent interesting. We will talk later, Kade is approaching." Kade got into the car, I twisted in my seat to face him.

"Thank god, your taste in women has improved." A small smile twisted the corners of his lips.

"Let's just say Clarice may have cause to dislike you."

"That was the first time I spoke to her, why would she have reason to dislike me?"

"She noticed that I was paying a little too much attention to you at Funmi's sixteenth birthday party."

"I didn't notice."

"You avoided me like the plague, and barely looked my way."

I shrugged. "You made me nervous." Nikki was right. I straightened my position and put on my seat belt. I glanced down at my hand and flexed it.

"How is your hand feeling?" He cast a quick glance my way as he started the engine.

"Not bad, thanks."

We drove the short distance to his flat in silence. I was curious to see his flat. We were in luck, there was a parking spot right outside Kade's building. We got out of the car and went to the boot. I reached for two of the shopping bags with my right hand. Kade picked up the remaining four bags and locked the car.

"Come on, I am on the ground floor." He entered the entry code into the door lock on the main door, I heard the click of the door release. Kade held the door open for me to enter first. Then led the way towards the back of the building. He stopped in front of the door marked "Flat 3" and opened the door.

"After you," he leaned back against the door to keep it open. I walked into the hallway. The magnolia walls looked like they were freshly painted. Underfoot was a beige carpet. It looked new too. "The kitchen is the second door on your left." I followed his directions and opened the kitchen door and entered. It was a good size with room for a table and four chairs. I placed the shopping bag on the tidy, grey speckled, kitchen worktop. Kade came in and placed the shopping bags he was holding on the table.

"The bathroom is the door closest to the front door. Feel free to roam around while I put the shopping away."

"I will pay a quick visit to the bathroom and come and help you. I can explore later." Kade nodded. His intense gaze followed me.

The bathroom was compact. The walls were painted a bright aqua. I did not linger. Washed my hands, taking care not to wet my dressing and returned to the kitchen. One of the bags I had placed on the kitchen counter contained fridge items. I put them away. We worked together quickly putting the items away.

"It's nice that your flat overlooks the garden." Kade was now taking plates out of the cupboard. Some of the items for lunch were on the kitchen counter.

"It is nice. I was lucky to find somewhere not too pricey in a good location. I'm surprised at how much I already feel at home here." I moved the Deli containers onto the table. Kade set the table. "What do you fancy to drink? There's orange or apple juice."

"Water is fine, thanks." He took out a jug and filled it with water from the tap and brought it to the table with a couple of glasses.

"Have a seat. Let me give you a hand with dishing the food." I sat down whilst he opened the cartons and dished food onto my plate. He then filled his plate. He sat down buttered four slices of the French loaf and placed it on a plate between us. "Tuck in".

"Thanks."

We ate in silence. I looked around the kitchen, avoiding Kade's eyes. My eyes settled on the clock on the wall, the time was 3:10 PM. It felt later. I peeked a glance at Kade every now and again from under my lashes. He seemed perfectly at ease with the silence. I was grateful that he was going to wait until we finished our meal before our talk.

I leaned back in my chair, feeling full and much better. Kade had finished the food on his plate. He cut another four slices of the French loaf and was happily eating it with butter. I smiled at the obvious enjoyment on his face as he munched away.

"You weren't kidding about your love for bread and butter"

"Correction – fresh crusty bread with butter. It's really good!" He popped the last piece in his mouth and wiped his mouth and hands with a paper towel.

"You have plenty of leftovers for lunch tomorrow." I stood up and started to close the cartons and took them to the fridge. Kade cleared the plates and placed them in the sink. I wiped down the table. He put the kettle on and washed up. I went to stand by the window looking out into the communal garden. It was already beginning to get dark.

"Tea or coffee? How do you take it?" I turned to face him and leaned against the windowsill.

"Coffee please, black, no sugar.".

He made the drinks, placed them on a tray and added the pack of chocolates I picked up

"Let's go into the living room." I followed him. The room was surprisingly large, yet it had a cosy feel. There was an accent wall coloured a vibrant purple. A large tan leather sofa divided the sitting area from the dining area which had a good-sized table. The dining chairs were the same colour as the sofa.

"Let's sit at the table whilst we have our coffee and talk." I sat down opposite him. He chose this seating so he could look me directly in the eye.

"This is a lovely room, it's cosy despite its size."

"Thanks, it's a good room to relax in. You won't be surprised to hear that I have some questions for you. Will you tell me the truth?" Kade's voice took on a quiet tone. Here we go.

"I won't lie to you. But some of my responses may not make any sense. I need you to take them at face value for now. I promise I'll tell you more when I can, I just need a little time. I also need you to keep what I tell you to yourself. Can you do that?" Kade nodded, his eyes fixed on my face.

"You knew that the dog was going to attack before it happened, how did you know?

"I sensed it. Let's call it a type of super active intuition."

"You sensed it?"

I nodded.

"Is that a normal thing for you…sensing things?"

"Recently, yes."

"You moved with incredible speed. I couldn't keep up with you, and I consider myself a fit person. How were you able to move so fast and is that a recent thing too?"

"I don't know how I moved so quickly. I felt a boost of energy and just ran. It was as much of a surprise to me as it was to you, so yes, it's a recent thing."

"How did you get the dog to follow your command? It should have savaged your hand."

"I willed it to obey me, I was not entirely sure it would work. I haven't tried it before on an animal."

Kade stared at me digesting my words. He got up and started to pace the room.

"You sense things before they happen. You can summon incredible speed. To top it all you are telling me that you willed a savage dog to heed your command. How did you do those things Brissy? Tell me how?"

"Remember what I said to you at the start of this conversation. I don't have all the answers you want. There's only so much I can tell you."

Kade stopped pacing and faced me, his eyes narrowing.

"But you do know what is causing these things, don't you?"

I nodded and swallowed; my mouth felt like sandpaper.

"Please tell me what you think is causing the things you described."

I looked down at my hands. God, this was torturous. I sat up straight in my chair and held my head up.

"I have a rare gene mutation. That's about all I can say at present."

Kade's expression might have been comical if I could see the funny side – but I couldn't. He walked over to me slowly took my uninjured hand and gently pulled me out of the chair. We were standing facing each other, inches apart. He encased my hand in both of his and looked me straight in the eyes.

"Brissy, what's really going on with you? Please tell me?" His voice was soothing and encouraging. I would rather he got angry. Called me an outright liar even. His kindness and concern were the last straw. The tears I had been keeping at bay broke the dam and started flowing. My pent-up emotions overwhelmed me. I started to sob.

"I know I sound crazy! You don't need to say it. I know, but everything I have told you is true. I am a freak of nature and my life as I know it is disintegrating right before my eyes. I don't know what will happen to me. Where these changes will lead or what is coming next. I don't have control over my life any longer. It's been taken from me!"

Kade said nothing. He just pulled me into his arms and let me cry. His hand gently moved up and down my back in a soothing motion.

I don't know how long we stood like that whilst I bawled my eyes out. When the tears eventually subsided, Kade sat me back down and placed a box of tissues in front of me. I blew my nose and mopped up my face. I must look like a horror show. I needed to wash my face. I stood up.

"I need the bathroom."

Kade nodded. I went into the bathroom, wincing when I saw my reflection in the mirror. I'm not one of those women who seem to be able to cry prettily. My eyes were a little swollen and they looked red and evidently unhappy. I need to get a grip before I went home. I washed my face with cold water. I cupped the water in my hand and held it to my opened eyes. I can't imagine what Kade was thinking. Actually, I could! Perhaps this would give him second thoughts about wanting to be with me. I dried my face and returned to the living room.

I hovered at the doorway. Kade had his back to the door. He was drawing the curtains; he had turned on a couple of the lamps in the room.

"Come and sit on the sofa Brissy, you look tired." Kade sat down and patted the seat next to him. My movement was weary as I walked to the sofa and sat next to him. He ran his finger over my cheeks. He stared into my eyes.

"The change in your eye colour, is it part of this gene mutation?"

"Yes."

"I'm sorry Brissy. I can see you are having a hard time. Sorry if I just made it worse with my questions, but I needed to ask. I can't get my head around the things I've witnessed. Something is certainly going on. But I don't understand why you think you have a gene mutation. Hell, I don't understand any of this stuff!"

I searched his face. No one would blame him if he was wondering which psychiatric unit I escaped from.

"No, I don't think you are crazy," he said, one side of his lips curled in a small smile. My eyes widened, and I smiled too.

"I thought I am supposed to be the mind reader."

"You think you read minds too?"

"It's more like hearing thoughts. Each mind has its own melody like voices. But I can't hear your mind."

"That's a relief. It would be a shame if I could never surprise you." He changed his position and pulled me onto his lap. One arm circled my waist, his hand rested on my stomach. He continued in the same even conversational tone. "I can see that ours is going to be something of an interesting journey. I don't get any of this stuff. But something odd is going on. I am an African man. The supernatural, paranormal or whatever you want to call it is engrained in my culture. We are told stories about witchcraft from an early age. I've never wanted to dwell on such things but that doesn't mean my mind is entirely closed to it." He suddenly laughed. "If I told mum this stuff, she would say witches are responsible and want to consult an oracle."

"You can't tell your mum any of this stuff. Promise me you'll keep it to yourself." My voice was squeaky.

"Of course, I'm not going to tell anyone."

"I can definitely say I'm not a witch.

"Good to know." Mirth glinted in his eyes.

"There's someone who has answers. You'll be told more but this is all I can share right now." I turned slightly so I could see his face and placed an arm across his shoulders. I said in a quiet voice.

"It would be understandable if you have changed your mind about us. If I, were you, I'd be tempted to turn and run in the opposite direction." He digested my words.

"I don't believe in running away from challenges. Besides, it is too late for me to run from you, Brissy. I am too far in." He leaned towards me and kissed me lightly on the lips. I closed my eyes relieved that he would be by my side for now. My eyes flicked open to meet his warm brown eyes. I kissed him. My fraught emotions conveyed. His response was instant.

His hands clasped my waist. He shifted to lay me on my back on the sofa, my legs on either side of him, he made the manoeuvre without breaking our kiss. There was a new urgency in the way his lips moved over mine. He kissed me like a thirsty man who had just been given a glass of water to drink. When he lifted himself off me, we were both gasping for breath.

He sat up and pulled me back onto his lap. He leaned his head against the back of the sofa and closed his eyes. He spoke with his eyes closed.

"We agreed to take things slow; this doesn't feel so slow to me." His eyes flicked open. "Brissy, it's important that we do take things slow. I already feel like the big bad wolf by pursuing a relationship with you. I'm older and should damn well know better. I don't want to take advantage of you."

"Are you saying we can't kiss?"

Kade laughed softly.

"No, it doesn't mean we can't kiss. I plan to kiss you, a lot. But we need to manage this intense chemistry we have. For the sake of my own sanity, I will take the lead on reining things in." In a fluid movement he got up and let me slide down his frame until my feet touched the floor.

"Well, that's better than how my dream ended, so I'll take reality."

"You have dreams about me?" He raised an eyebrow.

"Correction, I said 'dream' as in singular. I don't want you getting a fat head." His face broke into a big smile.

"What was the dream about?" I gave him a slow smile.

"Actually, it was a sex dream." He threw back his head and roared with laughter.

ഇരുണ്

11. MOTHER'S BOX

I woke up bright and early on Tuesday morning even before my alarm went off at 6:00 AM. As soon as my alarm went off, I got up, showered, and dressed. Everything else was firmly pushed to the back of my mind for now. I sat at my desk and studied for an hour. There were too many distractions at present. I hadn't invested as much time in my study and revision as I needed. I took a half hour break to get breakfast and coffee and returned to my desk. I worked for the rest of the morning. I completed my Business Studies assignment paper and fitted in some revision too.

I looked at my completed assignment paper and nodded with satisfaction. I would read it over one more time, make any final edits and submit it when I returned to college. That would just leave my English Literature assignment to tackle. I stood up and stretched, my arms reaching high above my head. I then bent at the waist, clasped my ankles with my hands, taking care with my injured hand. I felt the stretch in the back of my legs and my lower back. I held my position for a minute or so and straightened.

From tomorrow, I would accompany Marcus on his morning run. I felt a need for physical activity beyond walks. It would also give Marcus and me time together. Felt like we had not had much time to talk recently.

Second week of November; the Christmas season would be here soon. I love Christmas time. Not for religious reasons but rather the feeling of good will, and cheer that it seemed to bring out in people.

I heard the familiar ping of a message alert on my phone. I picked up my phone. It was a sweet good morning greeting from Kade. I decided to surprise him with a response in Yoruba. I had picked up some Yoruba greetings from Funmi over the years. I knew that Kade spoke fluent Yoruba. I called him.

"Brissy," Kade's deep smooth voice answered.

"*Kaaro, se o sun dada?*" Kade's laughter was full of delight, I greeted him good morning and asked whether he slept well.

"How sweet to be greeted so competently in my mother tongue. Your Yoruba is good. No wonder mum loves you like one of her own." I laughed, pleased with his compliment.

"Thank you. Aunty Bola is lovely and so is Uncle Jacob, they are my second family."

"It has fascinated me over the years to note how well you fit into my family. They love you."

"I love them too. Which nicely brings me onto the fact that I need to tell Funmi that we are seeing each other. Have you spoken to her about us yet?"

"No. Does that mean you have made your decision? You want to find out what is between us too?"

"Yes, I do. We will take things slow, as you said."

"I wish I could see you now. I want to kiss you."

"I wish you were here too. I'll be counting down the hours till I see you later. I'll speak to Funmi. She needs to hear it from me, otherwise she will kill me. Once I have told Funmi, it would be good if you could tell aunty Bola and Uncle Jacob. I'm going to tell my family over dinner tonight."

"Good. I am supposed to be seeing my lot for dinner tomorrow, I'll tell them then. Are you still coming over this afternoon?"

"Yes, around 1:30 PM. I have another hour of study then I must take care of something with Amada. I will then make my way over.

"Cool – *o dabo*." Kade said goodbye in Yoruba.

"*O dabo*." I reflected on the speed with which I was getting close to Kade, even needing him. This was not a comfortable place for me. Yet it felt right. An inner voice was uttering words of caution. Needing others meant exposure, which usually led to pain. But I want to do better at forming relationships. This was going to be my biggest opportunity and test since coming to live with Amada. I needed to be careful. But I would try to go with the flow and let things play out.

There was another important matter that I needed to address my mind to this morning. Amada had the morning off work, we agreed that I would open my mother's box after breakfast. I felt nervous and excited at the same time. This was long overdue. Despite all that was going on with me, I felt in a good place. I hoped I could cope with whatever the contents of the box revealed.

"It will be difficult. But it must be done, Brissy." I heard Soraya's words in my mind.

"Hello Soraya, why didn't I see you last night?"

"You needed to sleep deeply. You had an emotional couple of days and today is an important day for you. I am making good progress with communicating with you whilst you are awake, I believe you will be able to see me soon."

"Is it possible for me to see you whilst I am awake?"

"Yes. but only you will be able to see me for now. I'm not sure we will progress to the point where others can see me too." My eyes widened.

"We have some catching up to do!"

"Yes – I will speak to you later." It would be great to be able to see as well as talk to Soraya whilst I am awake. I could learn so much more. There was a knock on my bedroom door.

"Come in."

"Good morning, honey. How does your hand feel? I brought you coffee."

"Morning, thanks, my hand feels OK. I haven't needed the pain killers since the dose I was given in hospital."

"Good, such a horrible incident. Marcus has already gone to work, and Grace left with him to get a lift to school. It's just the two of us at home. I will see you in the kitchen."

"OK, thanks. I'll bring the box down in a little while." Amada smiled and left.

Sitting here obsessing about the contents of the box was a waste of my time. Best just get it over with. But first a quick chat with Funmi while I drank my coffee.

"Hi Brissy, how are you doing?"

"Good thanks, do you have time to chat?"

"You are in luck. I don't have any classes till this afternoon. I'm relaxing in bed sketching out some ideas. Is everything OK?"

"Yes, no problem. I just want to talk and update you on a few things." Now I had Funmi on the phone, I was not sure how to get to the subject of Kade, so I just blurted it out.

"Me and Kade are seeing each other. It's all still very new. I wanted you to hear it from me first." I held my breath waiting for her response.

"You can breathe, Brissy. I knew this was coming." Funmi laughed.

"How could you know?" I took a breath, relieved.

"Because my big brother has had a noticeable fascination with you over the years, from a distance. I figured it was a matter of when, not if, he would make a move, now he's back home for good, and you are now over the age of majority. I'm happy for you Brissy. I would say 'welcome to the family', but you're already part of our family." It would be interesting to hear what Kade had to say about the enquiries he made about me.

"Thanks."

"Mum and dad are going to be happy about the news. I will leave Kade to tell them. As it is my brother, you get off on telling me the juicy details. I am biased of course, but he is a good guy. You can take off some of that armour of yours. Let him in and allow yourself to lean on someone. It could be good between you."

"I'm going to try and go with the flow. I want it to work out for us. What are you doing on Saturday, are you free for dinner with me and Nikki? She's had a rough time lately, but she's come out of the other side. We're going shopping, then dinner. It would be good if you could make dinner."

"I'm guessing whatever is going on has something to do with that bastard – Carl. Glad she is doing better and yes; I can join you for dinner. I am good with whatever you guys choose, just send me the details."

"Great, I will confirm details by Friday evening. Thanks for the support Funmi."

"You deserve to be happy and to have someone special in your life. Try to remember that when you start psycho-analysing things. Don't try to talk yourself out of the pursuit of happiness. I'll see you on Saturday. Bye."

I finished my coffee pondering over Funmi's words. As I took the last mouthful of my coffee, my eyes drifted to the tapestry and painting on my wall. Some of my history was about to unfold.

I took the box out of my wardrobe and placed it on my desk. What I wondered will it reveal? I picked it up, balanced my mug on it and went down to the kitchen doing my balancing act. Amada was sitting at the kitchen table reading the newspaper. I placed the box on the table and took my mug to the sink and washed it.

"OK, I guess it's time." I sat opposite Amada and moved the box in front of me.

"Shall I go sit in the armchair, give you some space?"

"No, you're fine where you are." I opened the box. The first item in it is a vacuum packed multi coloured blanket. I took it out and placed it on the table. I quickly took the rest of the items in the box out and placed them all on the table. There was a photo of my mother and me. I was probably about six years old. It was in a picture frame I made at school. I studied the photo. She looked happy. Her arms were wound around me, her cheek pressed up against mine. Her long dark hair was in a braid. I was about to close the box when I spotted a letter at the bottom. It was addressed 'my darling Brissy'. I placed the letter on the table next to the other items and moved the box aside.

"Let's see what we have here." I pointed to each item. "This looks like my baby blanket. Her jewellery box, diary, photo with a frame I made and a key. I guess I should read the letter." I took a deep breath and glanced at Amada. She gave me an encouraging nod. Reached out and gave my uninjured hand a little squeeze.

I opened the sealed envelope took out the letter and started reading it out loud.

'Brissy, my heart, I am writing this letter because I know that I will not be around to see you grow up. It breaks my heart, but I know you are strong. Even at such a young age you possess great

strength and courage. That gives me comfort that you will be fine. I know that your journey will be a difficult one. I pray that you will be loved and will find good guidance, and support on your life journey.

My time with you is almost at an end. I will protect you with my last breath – you will survive, you must survive. The dark reach of my father has found us. They will be coming for me soon. But I will not let them take you. My mother smuggled me out of Egypt when I was ten years old to give me a chance at a different life. A life that is free from the evil and corruption that is seeded within my family roots. I was given a new identity and that is the life I embraced. That is the good life I lived with your father.

The last time I saw my mother and any member of my family was the day I left Egypt. I know she would have suffered a dreadful end at the hands of my father, for removing me from his control. As you know, I was adopted by your Nana. She kept me safe. She never knew why she felt compelled to do what she did. You will know by now that you are a Gene Bearer, and I am convinced that your gene will become activated. Your father and I are also Gene Bearers. We both come from a long line of Gene Bearers. Though we are Echoers, I believe your path will be different – that you will be a Mutata.

Your father and I knew that it was only a matter of time before my father's spies tracked me down. They have been closing in on me for years. Your Nana and I kept moving. Not staying in one place for longer than about 8 months. When I became pregnant, your father and I believed we would be together to fight for you and your sister.' I paused, my eyes flew to Amada, shock flowed over me. I looked at Amada's saucer like eyes, and drew a deep breath, my hands started to shake. I continued reading the letter.

'We had been working on a plan to keep us all safe. All we needed was time to complete our preparations, but we ran out of time when he died. Our defence was only half complete. I could not complete it without him. We had not been able to gather and store enough of the energy emitted from the special wave frequency we discovered. The energy we stored was not sufficient to protect both our daughters. The wave energy we stored to protect you both was only sufficient for one of you. I did not know what to do or how to fight them when they found me.

I was two weeks away from my due date when they kidnapped me. I was threatened and given a terrible choice to make. They found out about the work that your father and I had done to protect you and your sister. My Overseer betrayed me. She was one of them. I was given a terrible choice to make, I had to willingly give up whichever one of you was unprotected by the wave energy, and sign adoption papers, or be killed and have you both taken. I made the terrible decision to give up your sister. That awful deed has haunted me ever since.

Most of the wave energy stored in me that could protect one of you transferred to the first one of you that was born. That was you Brissy. Zahra was unprotected so they took her, I held her for barely five minutes after she was born. The only right they gave me was the right to give her a first and middle name, I called her Zahra Naomi. You are not identical, you looked quite different. Your skin tone is dark, hers is fair. Your hair is curly, hers was straight. She has a birthmark about the size of a penny on her left inner thigh. It reminded me of Saturn and its rings.

There is a small residue of the wave energy that you absorbed when you were born. It is all I have to rely on to protect you when they come for me. I know my father's men have found us, I spotted one of them yesterday. I can stop them and give you time to grow up. I pray that I am right that your gene will be activated. Once this happens, my father's options to harm you or control your life will be limited. You will have the capability to fight them.

I always knew that it was only a matter of time before he went back on his agreement to let me keep you. No doubt he's hoping he can persuade you with his lies. Groom you while you are young, and mould you to his will so you do his bidding. God knows what he has made Zahra into.

My father's name is Amon Gamal. He has an activated gene and is an elder in the council that controls Acadia. Your Overseer will provide you with detailed information about Acadia and Pro-Tego. Pro-Tego was set up a long time ago to help Gene Bearers by providing guidance, support and help to keep them safe. Acadia members were once part of Pro-Tego. About seventy years ago there was a split. There was a faction of Pro-Tego that believed that Gene Bearers were superior to the rest of humanity and that we should lead, and all non-Gene Bearers should simply be followers. Pro-Tego has always sought to live together with non-Gene Bearers as equals. The faction split from Pro-Tego to pursue their own agenda and became Acadia.

My great grandfather was part of the faction that created Acadia. My family have lived in and around the city of Alexandria for over a thousand years. I would have loved to discover Egypt with you. My childhood memories are good. My mother shielded me from the wider family. I even remember my father as a funny and charismatic man that loved me. That is the side he showed me as a child. But there is another darker side to him. The family gave my father the status of a pharaoh. His word is law; no one would dare to go up against him. My mother left me some information about him and Acadia. I have also gathered information about him and Acadia over the years. The information is kept within a safe deposit box. The key opens the box which is kept with Kendal Bank in Belfast. The password is the nickname I called you when we were alone.

Use the guidance and support offered to you by Pro-Tego and your Overseer. But you must proceed with caution, question, and evaluate everything, follow your instincts. The betrayal of my Overseer tells me that Acadia's spies are operating within Pro-Tego. There is no way of knowing how far up the leadership they have infiltrated. My Overseer was called Patricia Kane, she replaced my original Overseer in the early days after I met your father. I am certain that whoever authorised her allocation to me is also part of Acadia.

When they come, I will release the remaining wave energy. It will link with and boost the wave energy that you absorbed at birth. It will help keep you safe by cloaking you till close to the point when your gene is activated. You must find your sister. It will not be an easy task; my father will have poisoned her mind. I am asking a lot of you Brissy, but you must look after yourself, do not endanger your life to fulfil my wish. Zahra will not be like you. She was raised by a monster. If you can, try to save her, give her the chance to be who she was meant to be. This task was mine to undertake, but once again, I have run out of time. May God's mercy and protection stay with you, my love.

My heart and all my love shall be with you and Zahra. Peace be with you both.

Queen Sanura.'

She signed it using the name of the mother of a character in my favourite fairy tale. I laid the letter down on the table with trembling hands. I looked at Amada, her tear-filled eyes were huge in her face. I felt something wet fall on my hand. I looked down at my hand – I was crying. I reined in the sadness and rage I felt but I was struggling to keep my feelings contained.

"I have a sister." I whispered the alien words. Amada got up and wrapped her arms around my shoulders leaning her chin on my shoulder.

"Your poor mother, she endured a lot. It is wonderful news that you have a sister. You have a lot to wrap your head around. Do you want me to stay home with you? It's no problem to let Sandra know that I can't come in today." I shook my head.

"No, I am OK, thanks. I want to know what happened on the night my mother died. I still can't remember. My mind is a blank whenever I think about it. Over the years I haven't wanted to think about it. There's a lot to think about. I'll deal with it in digestible chunks. I still have her diary to read. That may give me more information and I will need to go and retrieve the contents of the safe deposit box in Belfast. I can't digest it all at present, one step at a time. What I need right now is some fresh air. I'll walk over to see Kade." Amada raised her eyebrow,

"You are spending a lot of time with Kade." Her statement was also a question.

"We are seeing each other. I was going to tell you all over dinner tonight."

"I like his family. I don't know him well of course but what I do remember is his calmness. It probably has a lot to do with his military training. As always, honey, be careful. I know you will be, but I need to say it anyway for my peace of mind." Her words distracted me from my inner turmoil for a minute.

"Yes, mama bear, I will be careful." She moved to face me, she put a finger under my chin and raised my head. Her eyes searched my face; a worried look settled on her face.

"I think I should stay home with you. The content of that letter was pretty shocking." I took her hand and got up.

"Yes, it was! But as I said, I will absorb it a bit at a time. You should go to work. I am fine, and I am not staying home." I really needed to get out, I could feel pressure building inside me. I had to contain it but was not sure I could. She gave me an uncertain look.

"Do you know what your mother meant by you being a Gene Bearer? Your gene being activated, and all that stuff about wave energy? It sounded strange and fictional, like something out of a sci-fi movie." I should have considered the possibility that my mother's letter could reveal information that I wasn't ready for Amada to hear yet. Too late now. I tried not to show any reaction to Amada's question. "Perhaps you shouldn't delay contacting Martha to set up sessions for after your exam. In case she needs a lot of notice to fit you in."

"I'm sure all will be revealed in time. Hoping to learn a lot from my mother's diary. I'll contact Martha." I hadn't lied, just avoided the question. She would never use the term 'crazy' but who could blame her if she thought my mother was crazy. For such a coherent person, Amada's thoughts came across as rather jumbled. I hoped she would leave it at that for now.

"I don't have to leave for another hour. Do you want me to make you an early lunch?"

"I am not hungry, thanks." I put the items back in the box. "I'm going to put this away." I left the kitchen carrying the box and went up to my room. I was starting to feel agitated. I desperately needed to leave the house; and get some fresh air. I was just about to return the box to my wardrobe but paused. I opened it and quickly took out the jewellery box, letter, the key, and diary. I opened my cupboard and removed my stacks of shoe boxes and popped out the false panel behind them. A surprise I discovered when I was 14 years old and kept to myself. I place the items inside the space and put the panel back and push my shoe boxes back into place. I also took out the framed photo of my mother and me and left the box in the cupboard.

I took a picture of the photo with my phone. This was the only photo I had of my mother, I wanted to ensure that I safeguarded it however possible. I placed the photo on my desk, picked up my bag and returned downstairs. I pulled on my coat and popped my head round the kitchen door.

"I'm heading out now, I will see you at dinner. Thank you for being with me when I opened the box." Amada got up and gave me a kiss on the cheek.

"Whatever you need honey, just let me know. Please do not bottle-up the things you have learned. I'll see you later." I nodded and left. My agitation was increasing and there was something different. I felt a tingling sensation all over my body. I walked quickly. Everything felt exaggerated. The sunlight was too bright, the cold felt icy and sharp on my skin and the sound of minds was louder than usual. The tingling sensation became more prominent, something was off.

"Soraya, what's going on? I feel weird?"

"It is the side effects of the emotional pressure you're under. All your senses are heightened. Remember I said it was important that you manage and control your emotions. The reason this is important is because whenever you experience extreme emotions, if you do not have the right level of control, there are side effects. Typically, the side effects are, violent feelings or heightened sexual responses. Sometimes it is both and more."

I was distracted from Soraya's explanation by a jogger approaching me. His well-proportioned muscular body was evident from the snug fitting top. As he passed me, I caught his scent and took a sharp breath. I turned around watching, he had a nice firm butt.

"Oh dear! I just checked out that guy's butt, this is not good! What do I do to get this under control?"

"I'm afraid you have to let it run its course. It should not last more than a couple of hours or so. Amada is right, you need to contact Martha. You need to get the ball rolling on your training, and Kade and Marcus need to be told they are Echoers."

"I'll call her tomorrow and try to fix an appointment. Maybe it's not such a good idea for me to go and see Kade in my current condition?" Soraya did not respond. I guess she wants me to make my own decision. What the hell, I am already halfway to his flat, and I want to see him. Now that I know what is going on, I can attempt to manage it. I'm sure I can do that. Ten minutes later I was pressing the buzzer on Kade's communal door. I heard the click of the intercom being answered.

"Hi Kade."

"Hi, come on in." I pushed the communal door open and entered making my way to his flat. Before I reached his door, he opened it."

"Hello."

"Hi," I responded as I entered and went straight into the living room. I could not sit down, I wandered over to the window and leaned against the windowsill watching Kade as he walked towards the living room. He stopped in the doorway; his eyes met mine.

"What's wrong? You're giving off a very weird vibe and your eyes look really bright."

The tingling sensation was becoming unbearable. I walked over to Kade.

"You know you never actually showed me your bedroom. You promised me a tour of your flat the last time I was here."

Kade raised an eyebrow. "My room is next to the bathroom."

I brushed past him as I left the living room and went into his bedroom. I heard his footsteps behind me. It had the same Magnolia coloured walls as the hallway. There was a double bed in the middle of the room with side drawers on either side. The burgundy sheets and duvet cover were the loudest colour in the room. A pine wardrobe stood in one corner, and there was an armchair in the other corner of the room by the window. I entered and sat at the foot of the bed. As Kade entered the room I patted the space next to me.

"Come and sit down." Kade's eyes moved across my face. He entered the room but did not sit. He stood looking down at me. I stood up took, a step to bring me a couple of inches from him. I closed the final gap and wound my arms around his neck and kissed him. At first, he did not respond, then I felt his arms around my waist pulling me closer to him. He groaned and gave in. My fingers started to undo the buttons of his shirt. I broke our kiss and pulled away from him slightly so I could pull his shirt off. My eyes travelled over his taut muscles and up to meet his eyes. I wanted to feel his skin next to mine. I pulled my jumper over my head and tossed it on the bed, my bra followed.

Kade drew in a sharp breath as his eyes took in my naked breasts. I moved in closer, so our chests were touching.

"I have a little problem that I need your help with." He cleared his throat.

"What sort of problem?"

"I am suffering from a side effect. It is creating a sort of pressure. I need a gentle release to rebalance me. Will you oblige and follow my lead?" Kade's eyes widened, he just nodded.

"What a gentleman you are." I whispered as our lips locked again.

About half an hour later, I was lying in Kade's arms feeling happy and calm again. Kade looked shell shocked but happy too. I kissed him softly on the lips and pulled away from him a little to lie back on the pillow twisting to face him. A wave of humour suddenly engulfed me. The look on Kade's face was priceless.

Through my fits of giggles, I said, "Kade, your face, it's so funny. Is there something you want to ask me?"

"Hell yes! Where the hell did you learn all that. I am seeing you in a whole new light. How does a girl who has never had sex know all the incredible things we just did?" I quelled my amusement. It was clear that whilst Kade had very much enjoyed himself, he was getting a little freaked out about my knowledge of sex and the human body.

"OK, what just happened was…" I searched for the right word, "out of character for me. I was kind of in a heightened state of sexual response, a side effect I did not know about until it was too late. The only way to regain control was for us to either have sex, which I am not ready for, or something inventive was called for. All my usual reserved behaviour went out of the window. Whilst I have never had sex, I made a point of finding out about sex. Call it the control freak in me. I hate doing anything badly. I figured I should know about sex and the body. Didn't want it to be a complete shock."

He gave me an incredulous look. "You studied sex?" He shook his head, then started to laugh. "What other delights am I in store for?"

"I think we have both had enough surprises and adventure for one day., It has been one hell of a day!" Kade drew me to him and kissed me.

"Are you going to tell me what triggered this ... side effect?"

"I read a letter that my mother left me. I found out that I have a twin sister."

"Wow, that is big. Where is she?"

"I have no idea where Zahra is, but I guess the starting point is my grandfather. I'm still digesting the news. Don't want to talk about it yet. Let's just lie here for a bit." I snuggled close to him. A wave of exhaustion cascaded over me. I would just close my eyes for a bit. I just needed a few minutes of rest. Then I would summon the energy and whatever else I needed to wade through the swamp of turmoil that my mother's letter placed me in.

ഇരുമ

12. CANDOR

I felt little kisses on my face, my eye lids, cheeks, and my lips. My eyes fluttered open. Kade's face was inches from mine, his lips curved in a smile.

"Time to wake up sleeping beauty." For a moment I thought I was dreaming again, then the memories came rushing back.

"I fell asleep."

"You clearly needed the rest, so I let you sleep for a couple of hours." I did feel better, centred again. My eyes roamed over Kade's face. I felt pressure in my chest. I cleared my throat and smiled at him. Having propositioned him and carried out my will, I now felt a little shy.

"Hi." I said, looking away from him to fix my eyes on the wall behind him. Kade didn't respond so I was forced to look at him. His eyes were full of humour. I groaned and pulled the sheet over my head.

"Where did that rather forward version of you go?"

"I don't know but she needs to be kept on a much tighter leash." Kade pulled the sheet down to survey my flushed face. "I felt like a boiling kettle that had no escape route for the steam. It's going to get me into trouble. I was leering at some random jogger and checking out his butt on the way here. My mojo was out of control!" Kade frowned.

"Does that happen often?"

"Today was the first time. It is a side effect of me getting excessively emotional. I need to get better control." My mind wandered to Martha again. I sat up tucking the sheet under my arms, all I had on was my knickers. Kade's expression said he had questions, but he did not ask. He was holding me to the promise that all would be revealed soon.

"I can see I need to keep a close eye on you. Please stay away from random men. I'm very happy to relieve your pressure." His statement was made partly in jest but there was a serious undertone too. He got up and swiped the sheet off me and pulled me out of bed in swift movements. I squealed twisting to reach for the sheet.

"You don't need to hide from me, Brissy." Kade's quiet words stopped me. He gently took my hands and raised them to his lips, kissing them. His eyes held mine, then travelled to survey my body. I had a lump in my throat. His arm circled my waist and drew me to him. "You have a beautiful body," his voice was hoarse. His lips brushed across mine lightly at first then he kissed me slowly and deeply. His lips left mine to trail down my neck to my shoulder. He took a deep breath, clearing his throat as he raised his head. "You should get dressed, otherwise we won't leave this room for another couple of hours." A flush rose from my neck to my cheeks, I nodded.

"Do you mind if I take a shower first?"

"Go ahead." I walked out of his room, conscious of his eyes on me. I spied my bag in the hallway where I dropped it. I rummaged inside and fished out a hair band. I gathered my hair on top of my head and held it in place with the hair band and entered the bathroom. I took a quick shower and wrapped myself in a towel and went back into Kade's bedroom picking up my bag on the way.

I was relieved that Kade was not in the room. He had made the bed and laid my clothes neatly on it. I took out the spare knickers I always kept in my bag and pulled them on. I had been carrying spare knickers since I was thirteen, after an unfortunate incident with my period. Nikki, Funmi and Khadijah rallied round helping to keep my dignity intact.

I dressed and rubbed a little moisturiser on my face and neck, released my hair and gave it a quick brush. I left the room to find Kade. My nose led me into the kitchen. Kade was at the sink filling a jug with water. On the table were two plates with omelettes, potato wedges, and salad. He spied me hovering at the doorway as he turned from the sink.

"Hi, I made us a late lunch, come and sit down."

"Thanks," I took a seat opposite him at the table. "You are very comfortable in the kitchen, did your mum teach you to cook?"

"She did. Quite rightly, her view was that boys and girls should be able to fend for themselves. She said that there should be no difference in basic life skills taught." I smiled, imagining the no nonsense aunty Bola teaching Kade to cook, clean and look after himself. The food was good. I ate with relish.

"You're a good cook; the omelette is really tasty and fluffy."

"Thanks. When we are done, I want to look at your hand. How does it feel?" I wriggled the fingers on my injured hand.

"It doesn't hurt at all and I haven't needed to take pain killers."

"That's good. You must have a high threshold for pain." I finished the rest of the food on my plate. Kade was already done.

"Thanks, you seem to always be feeding me. I would like to repay the favour soon."

"Good, I look forward to a dinner invitation, or you can cook for us here." Kade stood up and cleared the table. I fetched a cloth and wiped the table and kitchen worktop down. He washed up the items we used. He opened a stand-alone cupboard and brought out a first aid kit and returned to the table.

"OK, let's take a look at your hand." He sat down and indicated for me to sit in the chair next to him. I sat down and he gently unwrapped my bandaged hand and removed the dressing underneath. I took in a sharp breath; my wounds were almost healed. That should not be possible. I flashed Kade a wide-eyed look. He was busy examining my hand in detail turning it back and forth. He looked at me with guarded eyes.

"Wow! You heal fast. I haven't seen anything like this before. Your wounds have almost healed in barely three days. You don't need dressing anymore. Is this normal for you?"

"No," I said slowly, trying to wrap my head around it. "It's more than a little weird. I shouldn't be able to heal that fast, should I?" I cast Kade a questioning look. He shook his head.

"Please put a light bandage back on my hand, I don't want to have to deal with questions. I have no answers."

"Why do you think you've healed so quickly?" He watched me carefully. I took a deep breath.

"I think this," I wriggled the fingers on my hand and turned my hand back and forth, "is linked to my gene mutation. I will contact Martha now and set up a meeting, you and Marcus will need to come along." Kade took my hand and began to wrap a bandage around the area where the wounds were. He stuck the end down with some tape.

"Who's Martha?"

"She's a psychologist, the woman who has the answers to many of our questions on what is happening to me." I took both his hands in mine,

"All things considered you are dealing with this remarkably well, or are you freaking out internally and keeping it from me?" Kade had a serious look on his face, an intensity in his eyes.

"I am really concerned about what this means for you and intrigued too. I've never seen some of the stuff I've observed during the last few days. Trying to keep an open mind. But that's not why I'm not freaking out." He paused and took a deep breath. "This will come across as being too soon. But I keep having to edit my words to stop myself saying it so — I am just going to say it. I love you Brissy, I have been trying to deny it for about a year or so. I'm tired of denying it and I don't want to have to hide it anymore." I gaped at Kade. My eyes felt like they could pop out of my head. My mouth was moving but no words were coming out.

"I know it must feel like it's really quick for you. But it doesn't change the go slow we agreed on. Although that has been compromised by the events of this afternoon. I want you to know how I feel because I don't want to keep hiding it from you. My expectations are still the same. I want us to explore what we can be to each other, at your pace." I was still unable to speak, my heart was beating fast, my stomach tight

"My turn to ask — do you want to run Brissy?" I shook my head and responded in a quiet voice.

"No Kade. I don't want to run. It's just taking time for me to absorb what you said. You really love me?"

"Yes."

"When did you realise you love me?" I was having a hard time absorbing this. I could feel the familiar disconnection being triggered — my fail safe was taking over. I immediately felt a sense of calmness spread through me.

"Last New Year's Eve, I drove you and Funmi to your volunteer session at the Sunrise Care Home party. I stayed to help too. I was talking to Mary — we go back a long way as I used to volunteer there. The ever-observant Mary asked me why I didn't tell you that I loved you. I denied it. Mary laughed and asked why I couldn't keep my eyes off you. Later. there was a moment when you were trying to persuade Chester to dance. You managed to get him on the dance floor, and I asked Mary to dance. Mary asked you if she could cut in, she danced with Chester. I danced with you. She was right of course. My eyes had been glued to you all afternoon. I watched you as you laughed and joked with the residents, you made them happy. Your kindness and beauty shone. For a change, while we were dancing, you forgot to be nervous with me. You were carefree and relaxed. That is when the penny dropped about why I was so drawn to you, why I was failing at fighting my feelings for you. I finally admitted that I love you."

I remembered that day. I loved the fun and games with the residents and the smiles on their faces warmed my heart. He was right, when I danced with him, the usual nerves that arose when I was around him were absent. He proved to be a good dancer, twirling me round with ease, our steps well matched.

"I remember that day. Is that what Mary meant when she asked you whether you'd had your light bulb moment yet, as we were leaving?"

"Yes, I will miss Mary. Mum mentioned that she passed away three months ago." I nodded, feeling sadness as I too remembered the feisty and loveable Mary. We were both silent for a minute or so.

"Kade, I need time to figure out how I feel. I know I like you a lot but ..."

"There is no rush, and I am not expecting you to start declaring that you love me too. We have time. You should take your time and understand how you feel.

"Let's get you home." When we reached Kade's car, someone called my name. Kade and I turned in the direction of the voice. A middle-aged woman approached us, she was holding keys in one hand and a piece of paper in the other. When she reached us, she held out the piece of paper. I looked at her puzzled.

"Hello, do I know you?" There was a vacant look in her eyes.

"No, Brissy, you don't know her, I am borrowing her to deliver a message. I am Amon Gamal, your grandfather. I think it is time we met. In fact, it is rather overdue. Take the piece of paper in her hand and meet me at the Condominium Hotel in the city centre on Friday at 8:00 PM. I would say come alone, but I doubt that Kade and Marcus can be persuaded to let that happen, so – the more the merrier." I now knew why the woman had a vacant expression on her face, her mind had been hijacked by my grandfather.

"Brissy, what's going on?" The woman turned to Kade.

"Hello Kade. I hope you are taking good care of my granddaughter. Your father and I were well acquainted. General Diallo was an interesting man. My condolences on his passing. Please encourage Brissy to attend the meeting. There is a lot she needs to hear." I took the piece of paper from the woman's hand. I looked around frantically. Was he close by? She laughed. It sounded strange and menacing.

"Brissy my dear, you have much to learn, I am not nearby. I will see you on Friday." The woman gave a whimper and rubbed her temples a confused look on her face. She turned around and walked away from us. Kade was also looking around.

"Get in the car Brissy." There was no arguing with his tone, not that I wanted to argue. I got in the car and put on my seat belt. He put the car in motion, his jaw set in a hard line. I looked down at the piece of paper in my hand. On it was my grandfather's name, the hotel name and address, the time, and a room number.

"Please explain to me what just happened." Kade's tone was steely.

"My grandfather, or someone claiming to be him took over that poor woman's mind; and spoke to us using her."

"Can you do that too? Take over someone's mind like that?"

"I don't know. I know I can control minds to a degree so I suppose theoretically I could make someone say what I want them to say."

"Did he hurt that woman?"

"I don't think so, but I can't be sure. Hopefully, Martha can tell us more about how all this works." I was tired and didn't want to answer any more questions. I leaned my head back and closed my eyes.

"You should call Martha, we got distracted before." He was right, I had completely forgotten. I found her number and called her.

"Hi Martha, it's Brissy here, I was hoping I could get an appointment to come and see you." She had been waiting for my call. We agreed on an appointment for the next day at 6:00 PM at her office.

"I'll be coming with Kade and Marcus, is that OK?" Martha did not object.

"OK, thanks, we will see you tomorrow." I turned to Kade.

"We have an appointment with her at 6:00 PM tomorrow. I think Marcus will be flexible and attend if possible." Kade nodded.

Kade pulled up outside my house. We sat in silence for a minute, then he turned in his seat and stroked a finger down my cheek, I met his gaze. There was a strange look in his eyes.

"I wish I could tell you that this is as weird as it is going to get but I can't. I'm afraid you need to prepare yourself; I think there's a lot more weirdness to come."

"What about you, how are you coping with all this? You have gone from a normal teenager to having to deal with all – this crazy stuff."

"The term 'normal' isn't a label that ever really suited me. I'm good at disengaging; I'm getting even better at it. I need to if I'm going to deal with this stuff. Here's Martha's address and number." I texted the details to him and continued. "If I can, I'll get a lift with Marcus. If not, I'll let you know and come to your flat after college, we can go together."

"Come to my flat after you finish college. I want some time with you before we go to see Martha."

"OK, it will probably be easier for Marcus to drive straight there from work, so that works well. I guess I'll see you tomorrow." Kade leaned over and briefly brushed his lips against mine.

"Try and get an early night, tonight." I nodded and got out of the car and let myself into the house. I heard him drive away as soon as I closed the front door behind me.

ॐ

13. WOLF EYES

Woke the next morning feeling tired, with a woolly head. God only knew what today would bring. I nibbled at the inside of my lower lip as I thought about the meeting with Martha. I caught up briefly with Marcus last night. He agreed to meet me and Kade at Martha's office at 6:00 PM.

I stretched under my duvet and glanced at my alarm clock. I was supposed to be going for a run with Marcus in about fifteen minutes. I mentally connected with Soraya.

"Good morning, Soraya – how close would a Mutata need to be to hijack a mind?"

"Good morning, Brissy. It varies; some Mutata have a particular talent for taking over minds. They can achieve this from a considerable distance. There's a record of successful mind control at five thousand miles distance. That is highly unusual though. I would say about twenty miles is more the norm. There is no way of knowing the location of your Grandfather when he took over the mind of that woman." I was quiet for a moment. Thinking about him and knowing he was the root cause of the hardship my mother endured made me angry.

I got out of bed and paid a quick visit to the bathroom and returned to my room. I took off my PJs and pulled on jogging bottoms, a T-shirt and zipped myself into a fleece. I noticed changes in my body. Increased strength, stamina, and speed. I shouldn't have been able to outrun Kade. He was super fit. My normal fitness levels were very average; running was certainly not something that I excelled at. A little experiment was needed.

There was a brief knock at my door, Marcus opened the door and popped his head in.

"Morning, I can't believe you are actually coming jogging with me at 6:20 AM. What's going on with you?"

I smiled at him. "Morning Marcus. I feel a need for some physical exercise. Come on let's go. I'll take it easy on you and slow my pace." I gave him a cheeky grin. Marcus scoffed at the idea.

"That's really funny coming from you. Let's see what you've got." We headed downstairs taking care not to make too much noise. When we stepped outside, we were hit by the cold early morning air.

"Goodness, its freezing!" I said with a shiver. I pulled on my gloves and pulled my hoodie over my head.

"Once we start running, we'll warm up in no time." Marcus set off in the direction of the open green at the end of our road. I matched his pace, jogging beside him. When we reached the green, he jogged on the spot lightly.

"My usual routine is to run around the green five or six times at a good pace."

"OK, let's do it. See if you can keep up with me." I set off at a comfortable pace which Marcus matched and increased. I kept up with him for two laps. He cast me a surprised look when we began the third lap.

"You're doing great, let's push harder." He increased the pace again to what I guessed was his normal running pace. I had now warmed up. I ran beside him for two further laps. My heart rate increased a little, but I knew I could go faster still with relative ease. As we completed the fifth lap, Marcus slowed his pace. He was breathing hard, harder than me. He gave me a baffled look.

"BJ, when did you get so fit? Have you been working out in secret or something? You don't even look tired!" I shrugged.

"My fitness levels seem to have increased dramatically. I feel OK. Do me a favour, I want to see how fast I can do a couple of laps. Can you time me on your phone?" Marcus looked at me as if I were an alien and nodded. He stopped jogging on the spot, took out his phone.

"Ready?" I nodded, "Go!" I took off giving it everything I had. My heart rate was now pounding. In what felt like no time at all, I had done a full lap and went whizzing past Marcus for my second lap. I pushed myself harder still. I knew I was fast, much faster than I could ever have dreamed of running. I came to a halt next to Marcus as I completed the second lap. I was gasping for breath. I could hardly speak, I bent at the waist placing my hands on my knees, taking a moment to catch my breath.

When I stood up, and looked at Marcus, his mouth was open, his eyes bulging in his face.

"Well, was I fast?" He moved his lips, but no words came out. He finally gathered his wit.

"That was bloody unbelievable! You just flew round the green. Yes, you were bloody fast – your speed matched that of a top performing athlete." He showed me the time on his phone, my eyes widened – it was fast! Marcus gave me a narrow-eyed look.

"What's going on, BJ? How did you do that? It should not be possible. Many athletes train for years and never achieve the speed you just clocked. What the hell is going on?" He gave me a weary look. "You're not doing anything weird like drugs are you?"

"That's a lot of questions. Firstly, of course I'm not doping, what do you take me for! But I agree with you, I shouldn't be able to run that fast. Yet I did. I've been experiencing some changes. Apparently, Martha has the answers to both our questions, she's going to fill us in. How about a lap of walking while we talk?" Marcus nodded. We walked in silence for a bit.

"You know you can tell me anything BJ, what is it?"

"I have been experiencing some strange things and the events are getting stranger. Since I was thirteen, I've been having dreams that pretty much come true. Not every detail necessarily but awfully close." I paused. Marcus said nothing, he remained relaxed. I continued.

"I dreamt about Amada losing her eternity ring. I knew it was missing before she told me!"

"When we got to the restaurant to search for Amada's ring, we were told that it hadn't been found. I suddenly got a strong feeling that we should go into the Ladies' and I found the ring. It had fallen down the drain in one of the cubicles that Amada used." Now for the finale – I might as well just get it all out. "Also, I can hear the thoughts of most people, it's as clear as if they are talking to me." I stopped walking and turned to face Marcus. He stopped walking when I stopped. The expression on his face was unfathomable.

"What's your theory, what do you think is going on?"

"I have a rare gene mutation, it's responsible for the changes. Martha is supposed to know all about it." I watched Marcus carefully looking for a response that I could interpret. He kept his feelings to himself and his thoughts were out of my reach.

"Can you hear my mind?"

"No, you and Kade are in the minority of people whose minds I can't hear."

"Is there anything else you want to share?" I hesitated; I hadn't told Kade about the incident with Carl because it hadn't come up. But Marcus was asking me a direct question.

"There was an incident with a friend's ex-boyfriend. He hurt her and tried to blackmail her. I got angry and caused him to have a fit and made his phone explode. It wasn't intentional. I didn't know the things I thought could turn into reality. He's still in hospital, but he's on the mend. There was also the incident with my penholder, and I commanded the dog that bit me to stop its attack." I was afraid. I didn't want his feelings for me to change.

"I sort of knew about your dreams. But the mind reading thing and what you said happened to the ex-boyfriend, who by the way sounds like a complete asshole, is hard to wrap my head around." A perplex expression crossed my face.

"What do you mean you knew about my dreams?"

"When we were younger there were a handful of times you knew things that you shouldn't have known. A couple of times you slipped up and said it was just like in your dream."

"You are keeping a tight lid on your feelings right now. Tell me what you are thinking, it's not every day I tell you that I am a mutant with powers!"

"Well, I don't need to be able to read minds to know what's going through yours. First, I accept that all that you have told me could be seen as freakish but that doesn't make you a freak. I'm sorry that guy got hurt. But I know you wouldn't deliberately hurt someone." He took me by the shoulders. "I can accept the dreams as some weird super connection of some sort. But mind reading and having thoughts that turn to reality, that's hard for me to swallow. If you were anyone else, I would call you crazy or a liar. But I know you BJ. Clearly you believe you are the cause of these things, but there must be another explanation. A more rational reason than gene mutation. How did you even come up with the gene mutation stuff? Whatever is going on may look like a mind bender. But it's probably just some odd coincidence. Shit happens!"

"Maybe I'm crazy."

"You are not crazy; believe me, I know crazy!" Marcus' lips twisted in a sardonic smile. I knew he was thinking about his mother.

"I need you to keep an open mind when we speak to Martha. Promise you'll hear her out."

"I promise. She certainly has a lot of explaining if she put this gene mutation thought into your head."

"Whatever happens, I have your back, always." I threw my arms around him and hugged him tight. I blinked away the tears. His arms went around me.

"Thank you, Marcus." I released him and gave him a grateful smile.

"You didn't answer my question. How do you know you have a gene mutation; did Martha tell you that?" I kind of knew that was coming, Marcus had a brain like a computer. Little escaped him.

"No, I haven't spoken to Martha about this stuff yet. What I've told you is kind of all that I can say for now. Can you trust me on this for now?" Marcus' sharp grey eyes scrutinised my face.

"OK, I will let it be for now. But we're coming back to this. Come on we should head back. By the way, what's going on between you and Kade?" I gave Marcus a sideways look as we walked back home.

"We're seeing each other."

"I guess that was coming at some point. He's had a thing for you for a while. I respect the fact that he kept his distance when you were younger."

"You knew."

"At Funmi's sixteenth birthday party, he was having a hard time keeping his eyes off you." It looks like I'm the only one who had not known how Kade felt about me. "Kade seems like a good guy, but he comes with baggage from his time in the Army. Tread carefully." I nodded and changed the subject.

"I'm probably going to hurt like hell tomorrow. Can I jump in the shower first? I'll be quick?"

"Sure, go ahead." Marcus opened the door and we both walked in. I headed straight up the stairs and went to shower. When I returned to my room, I sat on the edge of my bed examining my reflection in the wardrobe mirror. I closed my eyes and took three deep breaths. My eyes open, I really needed to eat, my stomach felt like it was being squeezed.

"Soraya, why am I experiencing physical changes? What else should I prepare myself for?" I almost jumped out of my skin when Soraya appeared before me. I gasped, placing my hand on my chest. "You scared the hell out of me."

"Apologies, Brissy. I should have warned you." I got up and walked around her examining her. I reached out and poked her arm with my finger, not really knowing what to expect. "You feel real, but you can't be. Can you?" I whispered in shock. I shook my head trying to wrap my mind around this new turn of events. "Are you actually real or is it all in my mind?"

"It's difficult to explain fully. I'm not actual flesh and blood. However, your mind's perception of me gives me the attributes of a real person. My connection to you is strengthening."

"So how does this work? Am I the only one who will be able to see you?"

"Yes, you are the only one who can see me." I continued to examine Soraya. She wore the white gown again, her long dark hair flowing down her back. Her golden eyes looked back at me.

"This is beyond weird. Does this mean you can now appear in person when you want to?"

"I can take this form at will." I walked over to my desk and picked up my stress ball.

"Catch." I threw the ball in Soraya's direction. She caught it with ease walked over to my desk to stand by me and placed the stress ball back on my desk. She smiled.

"It's understandable that this is disconcerting for you. In response to your earlier question, a degree of physical change is not unexpected. I can take an educated guess as to what your body may be going through. But I must admit that I do not know for sure. That was a rather impressive display you gave out there."

"What do you think is going on?"

"I think the gene is improving you physically. Making you stronger, giving you more stamina, speed, etc. You will find that your muscles tone up and you may lose a little weight. I don't think there will be a drastic change in your physical appearance."

"I hope you're right. It's hard enough that I no longer feel like myself. It would be too much to also have a stranger's face stare back at me in the mirror. Like someone else had taken over my mind as well as my body." I looked Soraya in the eyes, eyes like my own. "I am in for a long ride with this transformation, aren't I? I feel mentally and physically exhausted, but I sense it is just the beginning." Soraya gave me a sympathetic look.

"Do you remember the path I invited you to step onto when we first met?" I nodded, picturing the white path. "You may also recall that the path stretched far into the distance beyond the point that we could see. That is your true-life path, it is long and not entirely visible. It is not like the life path of the average person. You are far from average. You are strong, you will cope. The indications are that you have the capability to excel, to stand apart even amongst the Mutata. Part of the training will be to help you increase your resilience."

My heart sank. I was just starting the race and I was already struggling for breath. I prayed that I would cope. One thing was clear, giving in to my tiredness was not an option.

"Thanks for being straight with me Soraya." I cleared my throat and squared my shoulders. "I must get ready for college and I want a big breakfast. My appetite is another thing that has changed. I guess it is linked to the physical changes. I'll catch-up with you later." I paused, giving her a curious look. "By the way, what do you do when you are not talking to me?" Soraya smiled.

"I learn - about you, those in your life, and about the gene, and I mine the CC Link. I will see you later – literally." She disappeared before I could say another word.

I dressed in jeans, a black T-shirt, and an oversized rust coloured jumper. I pulled on black ankle boots and went downstairs to make myself breakfast. Marcus was in the kitchen, dressed for work, shoving cereal in his mouth.

"Hi, my first meeting has been brought forward by half an hour, I have to run. Right now, I could really do with some of your mysterious speed. I await a full explanation of what's happening with bated breath. Martha will have her work cut out tonight. I have a lot of questions. See you later."

"Please don't be late."

"Don't worry, I'll be there by 6:00 PM." He grabbed some papers and dashed out of the door. Moments later I heard the front door shut. I glanced up at the clock – 7:50 AM, I needed to be at college by 10:00 AM. I made myself scrambled eggs, vegetarian sausages with baked beans and toast. I devoured my morning feast and sat back in the chair sipping my coffee and staring at the wall opposite me. My mind shuffled through the composition of minds in neighbouring properties.

"Morning honey, you were up bright and early." Amada's voice reeled my wandering mind back in. Amada and Grace entered the kitchen.

"Morning, Brissy," said Grace as she opened a cupboard and took out two breakfast bars. She put one of them in her school bag and added a banana. She picked up another banana and handed it to Amada with the other breakfast bar.

"Morning, I went for a jog with Marcus. Are you guys off now?" Grace choked on the orange juice she was guzzling down. Her eyes widened. She cleared her throat.

"You, jogging, voluntarily?" I nodded with a small smile. "No way! What has Marcus got on you to make you go jogging with him?"

"Nothing, and you needn't sound so astonished! I've decided to get more active, is there anything wrong with that?" Amada began to chuckle. She came over to me and placed her hand on my forehead.

"Are you feeling OK honey?" Her eyes were dancing with amusement.

"Thanks for the support!" I gave them both a mock wounded look.

"Sorry, honey. You must admit it is somewhat out of character for you to go jogging. I know you love walking, but jogging is new. Still, I think it is great, we are with you hundred percent." Grace gave me a sceptical look but nodded.

"I applaud your effort," said Grace. I narrowed my eyes at Grace, her barely contained amusement was audible in her thoughts. "Right, we better get going Amada. See you later Brissy."

"See you honey." Amada gave me a kiss on the cheek. I gave them both a bright smile.

"Have a good day," I said as I gave them a little wave. I was alone in the house. Amada usually gave Grace a lift to school. It was on the way to the Arts and crafts shop she ran with her business partner, Sandra Jones.

I washed my dishes, tidied up the kitchen and returned to my room. There's an hour and a half before my first class. I sat at my desk and picked up the photo of my mother and me. I traced a finger over her face, wishing with all my heart that she was here.

In the space of a week my life had been turned upside down and broken into fragments. Each one of those fragments was morphing into something unrecognisable to me. They were pieces to a new puzzle, and I had no idea what the completed picture would look like. I had gone from a quiet life; surrounded by love, hopes and dreams that were my own - to this. Now I am a walking science experiment. A dangerous and unpredictable one. I was thankful that I still have love in my life. The love of my family, friends, and the love of Kade.

Getting depressed was not going to make anything better. I simply have to take each day at a time and focus on the few things that are still within my control.

I retrieved the items placed in my secret hiding spot in my storage cupboard. I opened the jewellery box; inside were six items. I picked up a beautiful silver ring. The band was designed with leaves, a flower at the centre with a ruby in the pistil. A flash of memory came to mind; my mother had worn the ring. I tried it on the ring finger of my right hand; it fitted perfectly.

There were two identical necklaces, except one had a small gold disc at the centre and the other had a silver disc. I picked up the silver one, it was unusual. The cord was made of a charcoal woven material, the silver disc in the centre had carved geometric patterns. I could feel an engraving on the back. I turned it over. 'Zahra' was engraved at the back of the disc. I picked up the gold version of the necklace and turned it over. My name was engraved on the back of the gold disc. I rubbed my thumb over the gold disc, the metal felt cool.

The fourth item was a silver and black bead bracelet, it was simple and elegant. The final item was another ring, I instinctively knew that it was my father's. It was clearly too big to have belonged to my mother. It looked like it was made of jade; the thick band had a circular carving in the centre. I placed it in the centre of my palm; holding an item he had worn was the closest I would ever get to touching him. Tears slid down my face. I wiped them away with the back of my hand.

I placed all the items back in the jewellery box except for the silver ring on my finger. I would wear it. It made me feel connected to my mother. I returned everything to their hiding place and pushed my shoe boxes back in place. I stood back to check that there was no clue that there was a hidden compartment in the panels. There was probably no reason to keep the items hidden but my gut told me to.

I went to the bathroom and washed my face and returned to my room. I rubbed a little moisturiser on and packed my bag for college. I would print out my completed Business Studies assignment paper when I got there and hand it in. My bus would be arriving in ten minutes. I went down, pulled on my coat, and wound my scarf around my neck. I felt a cold blast of air as I stepped outside and pulled the door shut behind me. Going to college had a welcome air of normality about it.

When I reached the bus stop, I placed my bag on one of the empty seats and looked around. As usual Pershore Road was busy with traffic. I took my phone out of my pocket and began scrolling through my emails. Crap! There was a reminder from the University of Birmingham. I hadn't accepted my offer; the deadline was Friday. How the hell could I have forgotten to send the acceptance email? This failure spoke volumes. I forgot to secure the thing that was my biggest priority up until a few days ago. My offer letter was still in my bag. I would deal with it when I got to college.

I looked up from my phone. The bus should arrive in a couple of minutes. A Magpie landed on the roof of the bus stop opposite me. I watched it as it pecked at the surface. It clearly found some morsels to consume. Its black and white feathers glistened in the winter sunlight. It suddenly squawked, as if startled, and flew away. My eyes followed it until it was out of sight.

I frowned; I had the uncomfortable feeling that someone was staring at me. I brought my gaze down from the sky back to the bus stop. A man was sitting there. I did not want to look at his face yet. My eyes went to his brown shoes travelling up the hem of his blue jeans. Judging from the length of his legs he was tall. His hands were olive toned and linked loosely together resting on his stomach. He was wearing a smart black coat that sat perfectly across his broad shoulders. It looked like it had been made to measure. A grey polo neck hugged his neck. His chin was covered in a short black beard that linked to a neat moustache which framed a full shapely mouth. He suddenly stood up and my eyes flew to meet his. I gasped as I stared at the same golden shade eyes as my own.

My gaze was severed by the bus pulling up in front of me. I got on. Thankfully, the bus was not full. I quickly found a window seat. He was still there, his gaze met mine again. A small smile curved his lips. The bus pulled away, I turned craning my neck to see him. He is a Gene Bearer, more to the point he's a Mutata. Who is he?

I could not believe that it was a coincidence that he was sitting across the road from me. He had been staring at me. He had not been there when I arrived at my bus stop. His gaze was curious with a tinge of surprise in his eyes.

"Soraya, did you see that man?"

"Yes."

"He had the same colour eyes as me, that means he is a Mutata, right?"

"Yes, he carries an activated gene."

"What are the chances of me coming across another person with an activated gene?"

"The chances of you meeting another Gene Bearer are higher than you might think. Gene Bearers have a genetic pull; they tend to gravitate towards each other. It's not uncommon to find clusters living in close proximity to each other. However, the chances of you meeting another Mutata by chance are negligible. I do not believe that it was a coincidence."

"He made me feel uncomfortable. I think he's bad news."

"Try not to worry Brissy, focus on your immediate priorities. Have a good day at college." Soraya was right. I gave myself a mental shake and sat back in my seat for the ten minutes' ride. I got off the bus and walked towards the familiarity of my college building. My eyes roamed over the building, settling on the sign – Norton and King College of Further Education. This was my turf, I felt balanced and at home here.

"Brissy." I turned in the direction of the voice that called my name. Kate Thompson, a fellow student on my English Literature course waved and jogged towards me. I've known Kate since secondary school. Although we were in different friendship circles, we had always got along.

"Hi Kate, how are you doing?" I greeted her with a smile. Kate was tall and slender, her pale skin dotted with freckles. Her strawberry blond hair was pulled away from her face in a ponytail. She had the sort of face that I would describe as interesting. She smiled, her violet eyes twinkling.

"Hello, nice contact lenses. I am looking forward to the Christmas holidays; I will be spending it with my dad in Canada. How are things with you?" I smiled but did not bother correcting Kate's assumption that I was wearing contact lenses. Kate's parents are divorced; she lives with her mum and two older brothers. Her dad emigrated to Canada a few years ago and had remarried earlier in the year.

"I'm fine, thanks. How are you getting on with your book discussion paper?" Kate wrinkled her nose.

"Not bad. I chose The Alchemist by Paulo Coelho. I've read the book a couple of times. But haven't started my paper yet. I hear that Ben Collins is back, and that he is having a birthday bash next Saturday. I would love to go but I don't want to go with Trish and her lot. Are you going?" Trish and her crew were too open to trying everything for my taste in friends. I supressed a smile as I heard the colourful description in Kate's thoughts on Trish and her crew.

"I bumped into Ben a few nights ago. He invited me, Funmi, Khadijah and Nikki. I'm not sure whether I am going but happy to let you know. I should know by this weekend." I forgot about Ben's invitation; I would check with the girls whether they want to go.

"That would be great. I have a meeting with the careers adviser, see you in class." I nodded, feeling a little more light-hearted. I could occupy myself with teenage things once again, even if it is only for a little while. It took focus and effort for me to dim the lively chorus of minds around me.

I went to the library logged on to one of the computers and dealt with the acceptance of my offer. I then printed out my Business Studies assignment paper and went to my Law in Society class. I immersed myself in the rest of the day, blocking out everything that was not linked to my studies. The day went quickly. I grabbed a sandwich at lunch time, but hunger was setting in again. My Business Studies class was the last class of the day and it was coming to an end. I handed in my assignment paper and filed out of the room with my fellow students.

Kade's flat was not far from my college, no more than a leisurely thirty minutes' walk. I stopped off at the canteen and picked up a chocolate bar from a vending machine. I switched some of the books in my bag with ones in my locker and generally organised myself before leaving the building. No classes the next day, but I hadn't decided whether I would study at home or come to the library. I still needed to go to the Opticians for my eye examination. I promised Amada that I would call today and make an appointment. I would call when I got to Kade's flat. Hopefully, the lines would be free at that time. Eating my chocolate bar and listening to my classical play list, I set off for Kade's flat.

ಬಿಗಿಬಿ

14. ANOMALOUS

I arrived at Kade's flat still feeling balanced even though we would be seeing Martha in a couple of hours. I pressed the buzzer and waited.

"Hello," his velvety smooth voice made my heart flutter. I smiled.

"Hi, it's your girlfriend."

He laughed and released the door lock.

"Come on in girlfriend."

I pushed the door open and entered. Kade stood at the open door of his flat smiling, I smiled back. He took my hand as I reached him and gently pulled me inside and shut the door.

"How was your day?" I dropped my bag by the door and hung up my coat and scarf.

"All the better for seeing you." I said with a bright smile. Kade's eyes roamed over my face. He took my hand again and led me to the living room. He sat on the sofa and pulled me down to sit on his lap. He held my face with both hands while he kissed me deeply. I sighed opening my mouth and matching his urgency.

Kade groaned his hand slipping under my T-shirt to cup my breasts. We kissed and touched feverishly for minutes. When we were calmer and our breathing more even. I gave him a teasing smile.

"I do believe you missed me, Mr Diallo."

"God yes, I really missed you. You kept disturbing my thoughts and distracting me from the business plan I am writing." I laughed softly and kissed him again, I released his lips slowly trailing my lips across the scar from the corner of his lips to his ear. It dawned on me that I didn't know how he got the scar.

"I am hungry," I said softly into his ear.

"Me too," his hand stroked my breast. I gave a little gasp. I lifted my head to meet his warm brown eyes.

"I am hungry for food Kade." He raised an eyebrow.

"Are you sure that's all you are hungry for, Brissy?" My face flooded with heat and he laughed.

"Come on let's feed you. I thought you might be hungry, so I made an extra portion of omelette at lunch time and left it aside for you." He kissed the back of my hands.

"Oh, I need to call the optician before I forget. I still need to get my eyes examined. If I don't, Amada will insist on making the appointment and going with me. I know there's nothing wrong with my eyes. But she won't be satisfied until I see the optician." I got up and Kade followed.

"OK, you do that, I'll warm the omelette for you." I reached up and gave him a quick kiss on the cheek.

"Thank you." Five minutes later, I secured an appointment for 12:00 PM the next day. I followed the delicious smell of the omelette into the kitchen. Kade took the plate out of the microwave and set it on the table. I took a fork from the drainer on the sink and sat down to eat. He took the seat next to me. I took a mouthful.

"Once again, compliments to the chef." The omelette was tasty, rich with tuna, tomatoes, and onions with just the right kick of chilli. I offered him a forkful of omelette, he opened his mouth and I fed it to him. I ate the rest of the omelette in silence conscious of Kade watching me.

"How are you feeling about the meeting with Martha?" I got up and took my empty plate to the sink and washed it, my back to Kade.

"I've tried not to think about it too much." I took a glass, filled it with cold water and drank. I washed the glass and left it on the drainer. I filled up the kettle and turned it on.

"Would you like a drink?"

"Tea please."

"Look at me making myself at home in your kitchen. One tea coming right up."

"That's good. I want you to feel at home in my home Brissy." I got the milk out of the fridge and made Kade a milky tea and myself a black coffee. I took the mugs to the table. When I sat down Kade reached for my right hand and ran his thumb over my mother's ring.

"This is new." He examined the ring on my finger.

"It's my mother's ring, from the items she left me." He continued to examine the ring.

"I have the strangest feeling that I've seen this ring before. It's not exactly a common design." He shook his head, "I'm sure it will come back to me at some point. It suits you. You're going to have something of an emotional time over the next few days. There's the meeting with Martha today and then your grandfather on Friday. Try not to bottle up your feelings. I'm here if you want to talk."

"Thanks. I haven't yet told Marcus about the incident with my grandfather and the invitation. I thought it might be easier if he heard what Martha has to say first. It's kind of difficult to explain otherwise."

"You and Marcus are close." It was a statement rather than a question. I took a sip of my coffee.

"Yes. He knows me better than anyone. Marcus has helped me through some really difficult times. I love him." Something flickered in Kade's eyes, he lowered his lids. I realised that he may be getting the wrong impression. "Just to be clear Kade, Marcus is like a brother to me . We are close in a platonic sense." Kade looked up to meet my eyes.

"Thank you for clearing that up. It hurt to hear you say you love another man." I gave him a smile, leaned forward, and kissed him.

"Save for the pressure incident when I was leering at a jogger, there is no other man on my mind except you. Besides, I think I made up for my misdemeanour, don't you agree?" A small smile curved my lips. He smiled slowly.

"You were very …creative at making amends, no arguments from me there."

"Do you mind if I take a little nap on your bed for an hour. I need to shut down for a little while." It sounded like I was a computer, but the words described exactly how I felt.

"I'll come with you." We went into Kade's bedroom and lay down. Kade drew me into his arms, and I snuggled close to him feeling very much at home. His lips lightly brushed my forehead. I closed my eyes and drifted off to sleep.

It did not feel like much time passed when Kade spoke close to my ear.

"Brissy, it's time to wake up." He kissed my cheek and each eye lid. I sighed and opened my eyes slowly.

"It feels like I just fell asleep, what time is it?"

"It's five thirty. We need to head out in about fifteen minutes. Come on sleepy head, we must remember to ask Martha why you feel so tired."

"I'm also eating a lot more than usual."

"Noted. I'll remember to ask the question." I sat up and yawned.

"I need the bathroom," Kade stood up pulling me up with him. I went to the bathroom and washed my face. I also gargled with some of Kade's mouth wash. I pulled a comb through my hair and retrieved my phone from the kitchen. There was a message from Marcus confirming he would be at Martha's office by 6:00 PM.

"OK, I am good to go." We pulled on our coats and left. Martha's office was about a ten minutes' drive away.

"I'm not sure exactly how to get there. I think we will need the Sat Nav."

"It's fine, I know the road." Kade clearly did know where he was going, because we soon pulled up in front of the building. I spied Marcus' car; he was sitting inside it.

"Marcus is here." I got out of the car and approached. He got out of his car as I drew near. He looked tired.

"Hi, you look like you have had a tough day. Is everything OK?"

"Hi BJ, it's been one hell of a day. Some colleagues were given news of job losses, a couple were from my team." I gave him a hug.

"I'm sorry to hear that. You could do with a few days off."

"I have next week Friday and the following Monday off so I will have a nice long weekend." I released him and hooked my arm through his. We walked back to where Kade patiently stood observing us.

"Hi Kade, how are you doing mate?" Marcus shook hands with Kade.

"Good thanks, you?"

"Tough day at work, but OK, thanks." Marcus turned to look at me. How are you feeling about this?" I shrugged giving him a small smile.

"Come on, let's go hear what Martha has to say." I took a deep breath and led the way. Martha's office was within a converted town house with three other businesses. I pressed the buzzer for her office. A raspy voice responded.

"Hello, may I help you?"

"Hi, my name is Brissy Yah, I have an appointment to see Martha Maddison."

"Please come in." He released the lock on the door, we went in. We followed the signs for Martha's office which was on the ground floor. We entered the reception area. There was a young man behind the desk. He smiled.

"May I take your names, please?" We gave him our names. "Martha's office is the second door on your left. Her name is on the door."

"Thanks." I followed his direction with Kade and Marcus behind me. Just before we reached her door, I stopped and turned to face them.

"Whatever she says, please try to remember that I am still mostly me." My eyes flitted from Kade to Marcus and back to Kade. Kade took my face in his hands and placed his forehead against mine.

"Nothing she says will change how I feel about you." I closed my eyes briefly and gave him a weak smile. He brushed his lips against mine and took my hand. My eyes moved to Marcus. He nodded and squeezed my shoulder. We walked to Martha's office door, I knocked briefly and was invited to come in. Martha stood up as we entered, a welcoming smile on her face.

"Hello, I am so glad you could all make it. Please have a seat. Can I get you a drink?" We all declined as we took a seat. She had already arranged three chairs opposite her desk. I sat in the middle with Kade to my right and Marcus to my left. Kade kept hold of my right hand. Martha sat back down. She observed us for a moment and smiled again.

"I don't want to keep you in suspense, so I will cut to the chase. The purpose of our meeting this evening is for me to provide you with information. There are also facts about the three of you I need to share with you. We will need time for this discussion, so I hope none of you need to rush off anywhere."

"We'll stay as long as it takes to hear what you have to say." Kade responded in a neutral tone.

"Good. Brissy has been experiencing changes because she is what we call a Gene Bearer, in fact the three of you are Gene Bearers. The only difference is that Brissy's gene has been activated. I work for an organisation called Pro-Tego. We have been monitoring you all for several years, in the case of Brissy since birth because of her family circumstances. The purpose of Pro-Tego is to provide support and guidance to Gene Bearers."

"What exactly is a Gene Bearer?" Marcus asked.

"Gene Bearer is the name given to those who possess the Chrysalis Gene mutation. Less than 1% of people have the mutation. In a small portion of that 1%, the gene is activated. Those with the activated gene are called Mutata. Those whose gene is dormant are referred to as Echoers."

"Why have I been monitored since birth and what do you mean by my family circumstances?" There was a palpable change in the room temperature. My unblinking stare was fixed on Martha's face.

"Your mother was kidnapped by an organisation called Acadia, you and your sister were born whilst they held her. I think you know something about the story from the box your mother left you."

"You read my mother's letter?"

"Not me personally but Pro-Tego is fully aware of the content of your mother's letter, and I have been briefed on it." Martha's tone was factual. I sucked in a sharp breath. My rage was barely containable. Yanked my hand from Kade's and gripped the sides of my chair. Keep it together! I focused my attention on the silver letter opener on Martha's desk. The black handle had carvings on it, the blade end was narrow with a very pointy tip. It looked like a small dagger. It started to spin, slowly at first then with speed.

"What the hell is going on?" Kade asked as he and Marcus jumped to their feet. Martha remained seated her eyes fixed on me. The letter opener rose from the desk, its tip touching the desk as it continued to spin. Martha responded in a calm voice.

"I would guess that Brissy is having a little difficulty containing her anger." My gaze rose from the dagger to meet Martha's cool stare. I was surprised she was not in the least rattled. The spinning dagger suddenly shot through the air, inches from Martha's ear and embedded in the wall behind her. Something flickered in Martha's eyes, she quickly lowered her eye lids. Her face gave nothing away. Marcus swore loudly. I took a deep breath and forced myself to relax.

"My apologies, my control needs work. It's part of your role to assist me with that, isn't it Martha?" My voice sounded strange even to my own ears. I rose from my seat and calmly picked up the chair and carried it to the rear of the room, near the door. I sat down and moved my gaze first to Marcus then Kade. The same astonished look was on their faces. Though there were different questions in their eyes. "I have the feeling there is more to come that may upset me so a little distance between us is probably best. Please continue Martha." The corners of her mouth twitched slightly.

"Yes Brissy. It is part of my role to help you gain control of your capabilities. That display has disrupted the order of the information, I think we better skip ahead. What capabilities have you noted so far aside from that impressive display of telekinesis?"

"You should explain a little more about the gene first, to help Marcus and Kade understand. I know how hard this stuff is to believe." Martha nodded.

"The Chrysalis Gene camouflages itself, so it looks like junk DNA to an observer. This is the main reason, so little is known about it. The theory is that the Chrysalis Gene enables the brain to pick up the brainwave frequency. People and animals with higher level brain capacity naturally emit brainwave frequency. In addition, the Mutata can transmit brainwave frequencies on an incredibly wide spectra, and it can be targeted with great precision. The belief is that this is what allows them to influence or even control the minds of others. There is no conclusive reason why the eye colour changes. It is thought to be linked to the high level of neurological changes."

"This stuff is unbelievable, are you really saying that Brissy can control our minds?"

"No, Kade, not your mind or mine and Marcus' because we are also Gene Bearers. But she can control the mind of those without the gene." Marcus made a rude noise.

"Seriously, you are really overreaching now! The incident with the letter opener is … difficult to explain but mind control? Give me a break!" Kade was silent, I met his gaze. I didn't need to read his mind to know he was replaying the incident with the woman my grandfather used to deliver his message.

"Well, as they say seeing is believing. It would also be useful to understand how naturally this comes to Brissy. I propose we undertake a little experiment. Are you game, Brissy?" Martha asked.

"I'm not sure this is a good idea. I don't want to hurt anyone."

"If you are calm there is no risk to James. Are you calm?" I nodded.

"Good. Marcus, Brissy is going to summon my receptionist, James to come and ask us a question. What would you like him to ask?" Marcus frowned; his eyes uncertain.

"OK. Get him to come in and ask me what colour pants I'm wearing." Martha chuckled. I could not resist a little smile too. Kade watched us, a closed look on his face. All eyes turned to me.

I closed my eyes and focused on the image of the young receptionist. I felt a tingling sensation on the tip of my tongue as I made a cerebral connection with him and transmitted the command. I was surprised at the ease with which I accomplished my task. My eyes flicked open. We waited. It wasn't long before there was a knock on the door.

"Come in." Martha responded. James entered a smile on his face.

"Can I get you anything before I leave?"

"We are fine thanks James. See you tomorrow." He nodded. Instead of leaving he walked up to Marcus.

"What colour pants are you wearing?" He asked. Marcus' mouth fell open. James did a double take, his hands flying to his mouth.

"I am so sorry! I don't know why I said that!" His face went red. I felt sorry for poor James. I connected with his mind again and issued a command for him to forget. The expression on his face immediately changed. He smiled at us.

"Have a good evening," he said and left the room. Marcus looked at me.

"I made James forget. It's not fair to leave him worrying about why he asked you what colour pants you are wearing." There was silence. Marcus and Kade were looking at me with a combination of fascination and something else. I hoped it wasn't fear.

"You really can control minds," Marcus said. I nodded.

"Humans and animals – the dog in the park?" Kade asked in a quiet voice. I nodded again.

"What happened with the dog?" Martha leaned forward her eyes bright with interest.

"There was a dog attack in Cannon Hill Park. Brissy knew it was going to happen before it actually happened, and she got the dog to stop its attack."

"Unfortunately, that was after it bite a woman and turned on me. But the dog did eventually comply with my command."

"That's fascinating, not all Mutata can control the mind of an animal. The fact that you managed it at this early point in your transformation is quite an accomplishment." Marcus shook his head as if trying to clear it.

"Is this stuff going to happen to me and Kade?"

"No. You and Kade are Echoers, your gene is not activated. But Echoers do have a low level of some of the capabilities that is common to the Mutata. They can use some of the wave frequency emitted in their echo frequency with training. But I am not aware of an echoer who can actually control the mind."

"You should feel relieved; you are not as freakish as me Marcus." My laughter was harsh.

"You're not a freak, BJ. Think of it more as being superhuman."

"Brissy, what other capabilities have you noticed so far?" Martha asked.

"As you said, I can hear the thoughts of most people but not Marcus, Kade and yours. I hesitated before going on, "I also seem to be able to cause physical harm by thinking something. I was angry at a friend's ex-boyfriend; he hurt her and was trying to blackmail her into staying with him. In my thoughts, I wished he would suffer great pain and that a video on his phone that he was trying to use to blackmail her would be destroyed.

He suddenly had a fit, started bleeding from his nose and crying out in pain then he passed out. His phone also exploded. We had to call an ambulance. When I went to the hospital with my friend to see him the following day, he didn't know me. He did not remember me at all but seemed to remember everything that happened and everyone else."

There was stunned silence. Marcus and Kade turned to look at me. Marcus knew some of the story but Kade was hearing it for the first time. I kept my gaze fixed on Martha. I was afraid I would see fear in their eyes. Martha's expression showed surprise and – excitement too.

"Goodness! It is very unusual for you to be exhibiting that level of capability." My eyes narrowed.

"You don't seem terribly bothered that I hurt someone. Perhaps I could even have killed him, would that still have been fascinating to you?" My tone was sharp.

"Sorry, Brissy. Yes, of course I care whether you cause someone harm. But the man in question appears to be fine from what you said. The incident does show how important it is that we begin your training on control quickly. You must take great care with what you think and say. It is critical that you gain firmer control of your emotions. Otherwise, you could cause unintended harm to others, even kill. You will already be aware that you have more control over your emotions than most people. This control is a sort of fail-safe to manage your capabilities. As you train your mind, your control will increase." There was logic in the madness, my emotional dimmer switch was by design and not a defect.

"Has he suffered long-lasting damage because of what I did to him?"

"I don't know, only time will tell." There was sympathy in Martha's eyes.

"Why did he forget me after his fit?"

"I honestly don't know. The response does seem to correlate with what little we do know about the Chrysalis Gene self-protection traits. I think it is highly likely that you transmitted the command to forget you when the incident happened. It is also rare for you to have the capability to cause such a biological reaction in others at this early point. Have you noticed anything else?" There was an eager look in Martha's eyes that I didn't care for. I felt like a lab rat that performed a complicated task.

"My body is changing." Three pairs of eyes swept over me, I shifted uncomfortably in my seat. I cleared my throat and continued, "I am getting stronger and faster, and my muscle tone has changed a little. My appetite has increased, and I feel tired a lot."

"I timed BJ's speed this morning, it was incredible. It matched the speed of top athletes. If we, did it under strict conditions, I think she could be close to breaking a record or two. That's crazy!" Marcus said.

"I could not match her speed, when she tackled the dog in the park. She was incredibly quick. Is Brissy's tiredness and increased appetite linked to the physical changes? She is using a lot more energy so it's no wonder she is tired and is eating more." Martha's head bobbed up and down in agreement to Kade's theory.

"Yes, I agree. Brissy, your combination of changes and capabilities really are unique. I am not aware of anything like this happening, and definitely not at this early stage in the transformation cycle."

"How wonderful, I feel so proud. Not only am I a freak but I am notably more freakish when compared to other freaks!" The bitterness I felt dripped from my words. I quickly blinked away angry tears.

"I think your capabilities are awesome. Just think, you'll be able to kick my ass soon! I am going to have to train harder, and it's kind of sexy, superhero chicks are very appealing to most blokes." He gave me a wink. An image of me kicking Marcus' ass made me smile. Kade cast Marcus an amused look.

"I'm going to be working hard at keeping other guys at bay. I got that part covered Marcus." Marcus laughed and they bumped fists. Martha smiled.

"You have a lot of love and support around you Brissy, you are lucky. Many are not so fortunate. Is that all the capabilities you have noted?" I did not want to go into my premonition dreams, I nodded.

ഌേ

15. CHASING TRUTHS

"Something disturbing did happen yesterday. I had just read my mother's letter; you can imagine how I was feeling." I felt heat in my cheeks, I folded my arms across my chest. I needed to know Martha's take on this, so I am going to have to say it. I cleared my throat, "I felt a high level of sexual arousal." Marcus choked back laughter. I cast him a withering look. God, this is embarrassing, I sounded like a doctor providing a medical diagnosis. I just couldn't bring myself to use the word – horny! I could not look at Kade. There was a twinkle in Martha's eyes as she responded.

"That is a known side effect when your emotions are particularly unbalanced. When you improve the level of control you have over your emotions, it will mitigate that particular issue."

"Is there anyone you know of who would want to hurt Brissy? Someone who may be aware of what's happening to her?" I was thankful for Kade's intervention. The conversation steered away from my sexual appetite. Martha took her time responding.

"Unfortunately, there are. This brings us to another important part of our discussion. There are two organisations that will work against you all. Zraykus and Acadia. Zraykus are dangerous but their reach is not comparable to that of Acadia."

"How do Zraykus and Acadia know about Gene Bearers?"

"Acadia were once part of Pro-Tego; their members are Gene Bearers. About 8 years ago, a highly confidential communication intended for Pro-Tego was intercepted. This information was leaked, and a shadow group named Zraykus was formed by a man called Slater Samson to target Gene Bearers. Slater is known for having links to various right-wing organisations."

"A few nights ago, a man followed me; he tried to get close to me. He is a member of Zraykus."

"How do you know that Brissy?" Kade asked.

"My Guardian told me. She stopped him with the help of your echo frequency." A perplexed look settled on his face. I waved my hand at Martha inviting her to step in.

"All Mutata have a Guardian. Their purpose is to access and share the knowledge of other Mutata that is in the Cognition Cascade Link. It's a wave energy frequency that the Mutata can use to share information. Guardians can only communicate with the Mutata's subconscious mind, so only during sleep or some other unconscious state." Interesting – Soraya is different.

"Martha, do Pro-Tego keep a record of all Gene Bearers and their location?" Kade asked.

"Yes. We believe we have a record of at least ninety percent of Gene bearers."

"How many Gene Bearers live in the West Midlands?"

"Five."

"Four of us are in this room, who is the fifth?" Kade's eyes were fixed on Martha's face.

"I can't disclose that information."

"Why not? Shouldn't you be encouraging us to get to know each other, learn from each other?" His tone hardened.

"In theory yes, but I can't tell you who the fifth Gene Bearer is." Martha cleared her throat as her eyes moved across each of our faces.

"Initially, I asked the question out of curiosity about numbers. But now, something is bothering me about all this stuff. Marcus, you're a numbers man. If we round up the Gene Bearer population to one percent of the human population, how many of us would you say there are?" Despite addressing Marcus Kade's eyes did not waver from Martha's face.

"I'd say one percent of humanity is about seventy-nine million people. Proportionally one percent is small. But seventy-nine million Gene Bearers is a lot of people!"

"Thanks mate. As you say, it's a large number. If Gene Bearers were a threat, purely from a numbers' perspective, that would make us a material threat. So, Martha, how much of a threat are Gene Bearers?"

"Acadia is the single most powerful organisation. But there are lone wolves too that are a concern to Pro-Tego. Some have committed atrocities over the years."

"How did you deal with these individuals? Who decides their guilt and punishment?"

"That is not a matter for this conversation Kade."

"Really, I disagree! Then there's the ten percent unknown Gene Bearers. You have no idea what their agenda is. Objectively speaking, I can see how a group like Zraykus was formed and it wouldn't be surprising if their numbers grow rapidly. The unknown is an uncomfortable place for most. Fear can bring out the worst in us. Governments and security services of different countries will know about Gene Bearers. In short, each of us is a target. Acadia and Zraykus are not the only threat, possibly not even the most dangerous threat to us. Looks like that quiet life I wanted when I left the Army is not my destiny."

"I understand your concern Kade, and your background gives you more of an insight into the potential threat level. What I can say is that Pro-Tego has no intel to suggest there is another threat to any of you aside from Zraykus and Acadia. We do our best to ensure that any known disclosure of our existence is erased. Like Brissy, other Mutata can make people forget."

"This shit is growing legs. What happens if someone gets their hands on the record Pro-Tego keeps of all known Gene Bearers. Each of us will have a bull's eye on our backs!" Silence followed Marcus' words. The full ramification of what this all meant started to sink in.

"How did Zraykus know about Brissy? Her capabilities are new. You said yourself that there was no way of knowing whether she is a Gene Bearer until she started showing the signs. How did Zraykus get wind of her status so quickly?" Kade's question made Martha shift around in her seat and lower her eyes.

"The communication that I said was intercepted and leaked was about Brissy's parents, it named them." Kade swore.

"Zraykus have been monitoring Brissy and you weren't going to tell us. The risk to Brissy is material. Why would you keep us in the dark about that?"

"My instructions were to only share that information if I thought it necessary."

"Does Acadia want to kill me too?" I asked.

"They want to use you to further their agenda. They see Echoers and the Mutata as the next step in human evolution. They have been kidnapping Echoers for years and experimenting on them. Although an Echoer cannot usually influence the minds of others, it may be possible to achieve that if echoes of several Echoers are combined. Our suspicion is that they are doing exactly that, and that they target the minds of key members of governments and others in influential positions. Although we do not have conclusive proof, we believe that they sell these influential services to the highest bidder. The likelihood is that they have a new Mutata assisting them that we do not know about. In the last fifteen years they have grown exponentially; something occurred about fifteen years or so ago that gave them that leverage."

"Who heads up Acadia?" Kade asked.

"Vadik Romano."

My mind suddenly flashed to the man I saw at the bus stop.

"Do you know what Vadik looks like?" I asked Martha.

"Yes, we managed to get some images of him through some of our surveillance operations, but we have not been able to get an agent close to him. Give me a second and I will find one of the pictures we have of Vadik." Martha searched her computer files. "Here's one." She turned her monitor to face us. The man in the image was wearing sunglasses but it was him. It was the man at the bus stop. I gasped, my hand coming up to cover my mouth. They all looked at me. "What is it Brissy?" Kade asked.

"I saw him this morning on my way to college. He was standing at the bus stop opposite mine just looking at me. I was intrigued by the fact that his eyes were the same colour as mine. My bus arrived shortly after I noticed him. Something about the way he was looking at me made me feel really uncomfortable, so I just got on the bus."

"Good God!" Martha exclaimed. "Why is he here? It can't be a coincidence that he is here at the same time as your grandfather." I exchanged a look with Kade.

"What do you know about my grandfather?"

"Sorry, the list of what I have to tell you is rather long. Your grandfather is Vadik's deputy. Your family have been involved with Acadia right from its creation about eighty odd years ago. Control of Acadia used to sit within your family until it passed to Vadik's family about thirty years ago. Your grandfather's involvement in Acadia is the reason your grandmother, that is your biological grandmother, smuggled your mother out of Egypt. She wanted to keep them from corrupting your mother." I stared at her wide eyed, she knew a lot about my mother and her family.

"Please tell me everything you know about my mother and her family."

"We know that your grandfather is here and that he intends to contact you. If Vadik is here too, it must mean he wants to meet you. We don't have a lot of intelligence on the time before your mother arrived in the UK. Your biological grandmother gave the woman who brought your mother to the UK, you know her as your grandmother, instructions to contact us on arrival in the UK. We tried our best to keep your mother safe. Unfortunately, after your father's death Acadia closed in and managed to find her. They kidnapped her; she gave birth in their custody and of course, they took your sister Zahra."

"Why didn't they just take me too?"

"The wave energy that your mother used to protect you means that they could never control you, so in a sense you were of no use to them. Zahra on the other hand, could be moulded and influenced in a way you could not. It was a practical and strategic move for them to allow your mother to keep you. She would be sufficiently invested in keeping her promise not to try to get Zahra back because she had you to care for and protect. She could lose both her daughters and possibly her life, or she could keep and raise one of her daughters. It was an impossibly cruel decision she was forced to make." I fought back tears; what my poor mother was made to endure broke my heart. One of

Martha's people helped Acadia. Rage followed my sadness, I worked hard to rein it in.

A thought suddenly crossed my mind, Martha knew all these things about my background, and she was the psychologist assigned to me when I joined Amada's family. I gave her a hard stare.

"What did you do to me to make me hardly think of my mother until recently? Why can't I remember the night she died?" Martha sighed and sat down, a subdued look on her face.

"We were concerned that the trauma of what happened to your mother would overwhelm you, and cause you lasting psychological harm. Your Overseer before me was instructed to block your memories and when I took over, I was instructed to ensure the block was maintained. When your gene was activated, the block on your memory started to dissolve. That is why you are now thinking of your mother a lot more. In time, the memories of that night will come back to you, but there is no way of telling when that will be. Please be reassured Brissy, that we did what we thought was best for you at the time." Fury washed over me. I jumped up, sending the chair skidding away from me. A few steps took me to Martha's desk. "You and whoever the hell you work for had no right to do that to me." My voice was loud and harsh. Martha's face remained neutral; her lack of reaction only infuriated me further. "Who gave you all the right to play god and screw with my head like that? You had no bloody right to do that to me." I repeated and smashed my fists down on her desk. The desk shuddered under the force, then collapsed. Martha managed to jump back before the desk collapsed into pieces on the floor. All the items on her desk crashed down to the floor with the desk. Kade and Marcus also jumped up. My heart sank when I saw the look on their faces. I took several steps back from them all, afraid of what else may happen. Kade and Marcus took a step towards me simultaneously. I held out my hands.

"Please don't come any closer, I don't want to hurt anyone, least of all, either of you."

"Brissy, you didn't mean it. Under the circumstances we can all understand why you're upset and angry. Anyone hearing what we just heard would be," said Kade.

"BJ, you are still you." Marcus' soft words washed over me; I am still me. I needed to hold on to that.

"Yes, I am still me. Martha, I am sorry. You were simply following orders. The person who really owes me answers is whoever gave the order. I think we must stop the discussion for today, we do need to finish talking but not today. I will be in touch. Despite my reaction, I am grateful for your time." My tone was devoid of emotion, I nodded at Martha, she returned my nod and gave me a sympathetic smile. I turned around and left. When I stepped outside, I was hit by the cold night air. I started to shake uncontrollably; deep sobs raked my body. I could not stop the flow of tears. Marcus reached me first, he folded me into his arms.

"Do whatever you need to, BJ, to give yourself some relief, shout, cry, smash up desks. It won't change the fact that we have your back, you are not alone." Kade was standing in the doorway of the building speaking to Martha.

"Marcus, I can't go home like this, I can't face Amada and Grace in this state." Marcus nodded.

"If you're comfortable, why don't you stay with Kade tonight? I'll deal with questions from Amada and Grace. You'll have to call Amada; she will want to hear your voice. But I can ensure it is a short call. If you want to come home, I can find a way to keep them away from you. But you'll have to face Amada. She will want to see for herself that you are OK."

"Thank you, not just for today but for always being there for me." We hugged tightly; Marcus released me, keeping hold of my hands, and kissed me on the forehead.

"You'll get through this. You may even reach a point when you come to view your capabilities as a gift." I gave Marcus a watery smile.

"I'll stay with Kade tonight. When I've calmed down a little more, I'll call you and you can give the phone to Amada for me to have a quick word with her." Marcus smiled.

"Sounds like a plan. I am starving, you must be hungry too."

"I am ahead of you there," said Kade. I was just about to order from my local Chinese restaurant. I know what Brissy wants, what would you like?" Marcus put in his order.

"Why don't I pick up the food, and you can take BJ to your place? We kind of decided in your absence that it may be better if she stays with you tonight. Are you cool with that?" Marcus asked watching Kade carefully.

"No problem." Kade gave Marcus the address of the Chinese restaurant and his flat.

"OK, I'll see you guys in a little while." Marcus headed for his car. I watched him walk away. I turned to Kade; he was observing me an unfathomable look in his eyes. He pulled me into a hug and spoke into my ear.

"How are you doing?"

"I will live. I am sorry I lost control; it was a lot to deal with."

"You don't need to apologise. I was there, I heard everything you heard. Come on let's go, you will feel better after a shower and some dinner."

We drove the short distance to Kade's flat in silence. When we entered his flat, he ushered me into the bedroom. He pulled out a T-Shirt, socks and one of his jogging shorts from the wardrobe. He set the items on the bed.

"You won't win any fashion contests in these, but they will do fine for tonight."

"Thank you. I'll go take a shower." He nodded and watched me leave the room.

I stood under the warm jets of water, my mind a hive of activity. The tears started to flow again. I cried for all that I had lost, all that had been taken from me. My mother, sister and for the difficulties that Kade and Marcus would now have to endure. Because they are Echoers, and because they support me.

I finally got out of the shower and wrapped myself in a towel and went back into Kade's room to dress. Once dressed, I sat on the foot of the bed. I had cried enough, no more tears. I had to find a way through this, but not now. Right now, just trying to think made my head hurt. I heard Soraya's voice in my mind.

"I am sorry tonight was so hard on you Brissy, we will get through this. Do not try and get too drawn into detailed analysis tonight. We have a lot to talk about, but it can wait."

"Thanks, Soraya."

I left Kade's bedroom. I could hear Kade and Marcus talking in the kitchen. I walked to the kitchen doorway and stood there observing them. Marcus spotted me first.

"Hi BJ, I love the outfit. Come on in so we can eat. I am about to pass out from hunger." Marcus was his usual relaxed self. He was perfectly at home sitting at the table in Kade's kitchen. The table was already set, and the food containers laid out. Kade came to take my hand, his eyes scanning my face.

"You look better, come and eat." He walked me to the table. I took a seat opposite Marcus, Kade sat next to me. Kade switched some of the containers round.

"That's your order, go on tuck in." He pointed to the containers in front of me. I opened the chicken fried rice and spooned some onto my plate and added some salt and pepper chicken wings. I spied some mixed stir-fried vegetables and added some of that to my plate too. I ate slowly and watched Marcus eating with relish.

"This is really good. I'll be ordering from them again."

I glanced at the kitchen clock; it was 8:45 PM. I'd lost track of time.

"It's later than I expected, we must have been with Martha for a good couple of hours," I said.

"I was surprised by how much time passed too," Kade said.

"We can't trust Martha," I blurted out.

Marcus' fork paused halfway to his mouth, he placed it back on his plate.

"I think we are all in agreement on that point BJ. She's a slippery one. Why is the identity of the fifth Gene Bearer such a secret?"

"Maybe it's someone we know. But why keep it a secret?" Kade said.

"The other thing I can't shake off is how she was not more concerned about what I did to…" I paused wanting to keep Nikki's privacy. "The ex-boyfriend of the friend I mentioned. I am also angry as hell that they let my mother down, she ended up giving birth to me and my sister as a captive of Acadia. It also made me uncomfortable how she was positively gushing with delight over my capabilities. Maybe it's more those who she is taking her orders from than her that I don't trust."

"I am still trying to wrap my head around what we were told. I will have my own questions once I have had more time to digest it all." Marcus said as he raked a hand through his hair.

"I'm concerned that Vadik was stalking Brissy. Whatever the hell he wants, it can't be good news, if Martha's description of Acadia is anything to go by." Kade rubbed his hand over his head. A gesture I was beginning to recognise as one of worry.

"I am really sorry that your lives are being turned upside down. It's a crappy feeling – I know. We should talk about what all this means for you both." Kade gave me a brief smile.

"That's part of the problem Brissy, none of us really know what this means. Let's focus on the necessaries for now."

"Kade's right. I don't know how I feel. I haven't fully absorbed it all yet. Leave it alone for now."

"OK. There's still the meeting with my grandfather on Friday. Marcus, I wanted us to hear what Martha had to say before telling you about it. My grandfather hijacked the mind of some poor woman yesterday and made her deliver a message for him. He wants us to attend a meeting with him on Friday at 8:00 PM."

"This is the same guy who did or allowed those awful things to happen to your mother? Why the hell would you meet with him, BJ? What if it's some sort of trap to kidnap you?"

"We have to meet with him Marcus. He's the only one who can tell me where Zahra is. I have to try and find her." Marcus looked sceptical but nodded his agreement. "I want us to finish the conversation with Martha before we attend the meeting. It's interesting that she thinks that Vadik wants to meet me. There's a good chance that he will be at the meeting. I will tell her about the meeting, let's see what she has to say. The more we find out about my grandfather before we meet him the better. We only have tomorrow if we are going to finish the conversation with Martha. In the morning, I'll send her a text message asking for a meeting tomorrow evening. If I mention that we have a meeting with my grandfather, she will make time to see us."

"I'm coming to the meeting with your grandfather," Marcus said. I nodded, giving him a grateful smile. "It's a shame you can't tell when someone is lying. Maybe if I get you a lasso you can give it a go?"

"I'll work on it." I laughed at Marcus' comment. "Kade, any chance you have something sweet? I have a craving for sugar." Kade chuckled, he looked into my eyes, smiled, and leaned forward to gently brush his lips against mine.

"I see you are feeling more like yourself again. Something sweet is coming right up, I still have the chocolates we bought on our shopping trip." He got up taking our plates with him. Marcus made a move to stand and help him. "Relax Marcus, I am good." Marcus leaned back in his chair his arms crossed over his chest. A devilish look on his face as he waggled his eyebrows at me. Colour flooded my cheeks; I gave him a look that said I would kill him slowly later. I got up and started closing the food containers.

"I think Mui gave us extra-large portions, there is still loads of food left. You should take your leftovers home Marcus; you could have it for lunch tomorrow."

"Thanks, will do."

"How about some tea? I will make us peppermint tea Marcus. Kade, do you want a cup of your milky tea?"

"Sure, thanks." I busied myself clearing the table and made the tea. It occurred to me that Kade and I looked like a normal couple entertaining a guest. The idea gave me a warm feeling inside.

I placed Marcus' leftovers in the bag the food came in and stowed mine and Kade's in the fridge. I made the drinks and returned to the table with them. Kade found the chocolates. I opened a pack and popped a piece into my mouth, relishing the creamy sweetness as it melted on my tongue. I stared at the table absentmindedly tracing a pattern on it with my forefinger. I wondered what Zahra's life was like, what she was like. When I did find her, how would she react to me? Would she resent me for being born first? My life could so easily have been hers and hers mine. Chance decided our fates. I prayed that we could be real sisters to each other. That we would come together to dispense with all that threatened the life we wanted. I heard Kade's voice calling me, my head snapped up.

"Brissy!"

"Yes?" I looked at Kade, his brow was creased in a frown his jaw set, lips tight. My eyes flitted to Marcus, there was a worried look on his face.

"What's wrong?"

"Look at the table Brissy," Kade said. I looked down. I gasped, my finger somehow carved Zahra's birthmark into the wood. "How did I do that?"

"You didn't seem to hear us; we called your name three times. The end of your finger started to glow with some sort of energy, and you carved that symbol into the table. Do you feel OK?" Kade's voice sounded husky like his throat was sore.

"I am fine." I lifted my hands off the table to fully examine the carving. I was thinking about Zahra, but I had no clue how I carved her birthmark into the table. I looked at my fingers looking for traces of what caused this. There was nothing there.

"Sorry Kade, I've ruined your table."

"Forget the damn table. Do you know how you did that, has anything like that happened before?" I shook my head. "Do you recognise the symbol you carved, what were you thinking of just now?" Kade fired questions at me.

"Yes, I do recognise the symbol. I was thinking of Zahra."

"It's a birthmark." Marcus responded in a quiet voice. Kade and I looked at him in surprise. I had of course told Marcus about my mother's letter. He knew about Zahra, but I hadn't mentioned her birthmark - I was certain.

"Marcus, how do you know it's a birthmark, have you seen it before." I asked in a shaky voice. His face was white, he pushed his hand through his hair.

"Yes, I have seen it before, on the thigh of a girl I was involved with a few months ago." I stared at him wide eyed, my brain felt sluggish, as it struggled to absorb his words. Marcus knew Zahra. I did not believe for a second that it was some other random girl, it had to be her.

"You know Zahra, you know my sister?" My voice was so faint it was barely audible. Marcus took a deep breath.

"I knew her as Naomi, she came on a three-month secondment from one of our clients based in Egypt. We had a bit of a fling that lasted a couple of months. She left three months ago. I've not heard from her since she left."

"Marcus, think carefully. Do you remember which client she came from? What did you talk about with her?" Kade asked. Marcus stood up.

"Shit! The client's name is Capricorn, its parent company is Acadia Holdings!" Kade and I drew in a sharp breath. Marcus began to pace up and down the kitchen. A look of alarm spread across his face.

"Brissy, you met her briefly. Remember the day you bumped into me at It's a Coffee Thing? She was with me and I introduced you." Dear God, I remembered that day. Marcus and his companion were leaving as I was arriving. The girl with Marcus had been tall and slender with long straight black hair that reached the middle of her back. Her skin was much fairer than mine. I remembered an intensity in her hazel eyes – eyes like my mother's eyes!

"Oh my God, that was Zahra. I met my sister and didn't even know it! Did she ask you about me?" Marcus took his seat again, he reached for my hand. He was quiet for a moment.

"She did, as we walked back to the office, she was full of questions about my family – about you. She told me that her parents died when she was a baby and that she had been raised by relatives."

"She got close to you but never made direct contact with me, why?"

"We have to consider the probability that she was sent by Acadia to get close to Marcus and find out what she could about you. How did you spend your time with her Marcus? Kade asked.

"Other than the obvious." My tone was sarcastic, I threw Marcus a withering look.

"Hey, come on BJ. I clearly didn't know she is your sister; you can't get mad at me. She was just a pretty girl who was very friendly. To be honest, I was immersed in a tricky project, I worked lots of late nights, she was assisting with some elements of it but was not part of the main project team. We would grab a bite to eat together after late nights at work and then we would go back to her flat."

"Do you have a picture of her?" I really hoped he would say 'yes'.

"No, but there was a picture taken at a celebration dinner when the project was delivered, she was in it. I will snap a shot of it on my phone when I get to work tomorrow. This is getting a little edgy, it's beginning to feel like we are characters in a thriller film."

"I know what you mean, it's all quite unreal. I don't want to share this information with Martha. I want to meet with my grandfather first, look him in the eye and ask where Zahra is." Marcus stood up pulling me up with him.

"I'd better head home, I need to talk to Amada, and you still need to call and speak to her." I nodded.

"'ll see you out."

"Kade, thanks mate, I'll see you tomorrow."

"No worries Marcus, see you tomorrow." We left Kade in the kitchen. When we got to the door Marcus turned and took me by the shoulders. His eyes searched my face.

"Please don't be angry with me BJ. You know I didn't know who she was."

"Sorry, Marcus, that was unfair of me. I am not angry, everything is so crazy, then there is another layer of crazy placed on top. You didn't do anything wrong." Marcus gave me a hug and a kiss on the cheek and left.

଼ଓଓ଼

16. ZAHRA

I returned to the kitchen to find Kade washing up. The table was already cleared, and the kitchen counter cleaned, there was nothing else to do. I stood in the doorway observing him. I wished I could read his mind. What did he really think of the situation, of me? Loving someone didn't mean that person was good for you. I had to consider the possibility that I may not be good for Kade.

He completed his task and turned to face me, leaning his back against the sink area. He dried his hand on a kitchen towel and hung the towel to dry.

"You said classical music helps you to unwind. I think we could both do with something to help us relax. What would you like to listen to?"

"Vivaldi's Four Seasons please."

We went into the living room and sat on the sofa. Kade asked his virtual assistant AI to play Vivaldi's Four Seasons.

He drew me close to him. I placed my head on his lap and curled my legs up on the sofa. One of his hands rested on my hip and the other stroked my hair. The orchestral music filled the room, I took a deep breath and closed my eyes as the song of the violin solo piece flowed over me. It was like a wave of order flowing over a land of chaos. It washed away the discord and anxiety, reinstating serenity. We listened for the forty-three minutes it takes to hear all four concerti. I sighed as the music faded.

"Brissy, are you asleep?" Kade asked in a soft voice. My eyes flickered open, and I smiled.

"No, just very relaxed." I shifted my head and position, so I was lying looking up at him. "Tell me Kade, if you had not been pulled into this mess, what would you be doing? I know you would be working on furthering your business plans but what else?"

"I would be planning a four-week trip, to various European countries. I like travelling but have not had much opportunity to do it for pleasure. I would start my trips in Europe working my way up to a three months' trip to include countries like Costa Rica, Cuba, China, and Japan. I'm also planning to go to Nigeria in the summer for three weeks. The intention is to plan my trip so that I can spend about ten days visiting Kenya and Ethiopia before returning home." He smiled at me his face animated.

"That sounds really nice, Kade. You should still prioritise your travel plans as well as your business goals. Don't let this mess distract you from what's important to you. Right now, I see my dreams of going to university being eroded. I'm coming to terms with the fact that my life going forward is not going to be what thought it would be. I'm not going to cry about it anymore. I'm trying to look on the bright side. My hope is that these capabilities give me the chance to make a difference in a good way. I just don't know what that looks like exactly yet." I could hear my phone ringing; it was probably Marcus – time for me to speak to Amada.

"That's probably Marcus." I got up and went to the kitchen where I left it. Five minutes later I returned to the living room. "I owe Marcus one. I'm not sure what he told Amada, but she didn't give me the third degree, she just wanted to make sure I am OK. I thought she would kick up a fuss about me spending the night at your flat. She said she wasn't entirely comfortable with it, but she knows things are difficult for me right now, that if it helps me, she accepts it."

"Good, that's a relief. Hopefully, that means she's not going to treat me like the big bad wolf who corrupted her little lamb, the next time I see her."

"My mother and Amada raised me to think for myself, I am not easily corrupted." I smiled, "I need sleep, time for me to turn in. I am going to brush my teeth." Kade watched me as I rustled through my bag and produced a toothbrush and toothpaste." He shook his head.

"It never ceases to amaze me what women carry around in their bags."

"I always carry toothbrush, toothpaste and spare knickers." Kade raised an eyebrow.

"Get your mind out of the gutter. There's a good reason why I carry spare knickers." He waited expectantly, "I'm not telling you, it's none of your business." I heard him chuckling as I went to the bathroom to brush my teeth.

I returned to the living room to find Kade with his head leaning back against the sofa, eyes closed. I padded soundlessly over to the sofa and sat on the arm and softly brushed my lips against his. I lifted my head, my face inches from his. His eyes flickered open to meet my eyes. I cleared my throat and sat up straight. He lifted his head, not taking his eyes off me.

"I'm going to sleep in your spare room tonight. My capabilities feel unpredictable right now. It's better if I sleep alone tonight." There was a weary look in Kade's eyes. He rubbed his hands over his face.

"Sure, whatever works for you. The bed is made up."

"You look tired, you should get some rest too. I'll head home in the morning, give you time to yourself before we have to meet with Martha again." I felt terrible for monopolising his time and making him feel worried.

"You know you are welcome, here. I don't feel a need to be away from you or for general alone time. But you are right, I am tired, the last few hours have been intense." I nodded, again feeling remorseful that he was mixed up in this.

"Good night, I'll see you in the morning." I was about to stand up, Kade's arm circled my waist and pulled me onto his lap.

"Before you go, I would like a proper good night kiss please." His eyes lingered on my lips before rising to meet my gaze."

"Was the kiss I just gave you not a proper good night kiss?"

"Not the sort that is called for right now. Have another go." His lips curved slightly. I watched him for a moment my eyes roaming over his face. Well, if a sizzling good night kiss is what he wanted, I could certainly oblige him, with pleasure. I lowered my head and stopped just shy of touching his lips. I slowly traced the line where his lips met with the tip of my tongue. He sighed and parted his lips slightly. I leaned in my tongue slipping into his mouth, my body pressed against him as I kissed him deeply. Kade groaned and pulled me tighter still to him. On and on went our kiss until we were forced apart by the need for air.

Every part of me felt like a live wire. Our chests rose and fell quickly. I licked my kiss bruised lips, Kade's eyes followed the movement a sensual look in his eyes.

"Was that a proper good night kiss?"

"Go to the top of the class Brissy Jayne Yah." Kade gave me a slow smile, his eyes conveyed what I felt.

"Come on, let's go to bed." I tugged at Kade's hand to release my waist.

"Would love to!" I laughed.

"Our separate beds, steady goes it, remember?"

"I've been failing at that miserably. I want you. There is no hiding that fact but no pressure."

I kissed him on the cheek and stood up.

"See you in the morning." Kade nodded, I gave him a little smile and left the room. I opened the door of the spare room and stood in the doorway for a moment. I hadn't actually been in the room before. It was decorated in neutral tones, giving additional accent to the vivid shade of the yellow sheets and duvet cover on the bed.

I walked in and shut the door. I crawled under the duvet, grateful that today was almost in the past. Before my eyes drifted closed, I connected with Soraya.

"We need to talk but I am too exhausted to keep my eyes open. Let's talk in the morning. Good night."

"OK, good night, Brissy."

I was surrounded by thick fog, I could not see in any direction, there was a chill in the air. The memory of me falling asleep in Kade's spare room was still clear. I was dreaming. I could feel the presence of someone else there. I moved forward cautiously my arms outstretched in front of me. I heard the whisper of voices, I stopped in my tracks.

A beam of light pierced through the fog; the wisplike figures of two people appeared. The images shifted phasing in and out. The man had his back to me, he was holding a young girl by the shoulders, her head was bowed.

"Hafida, it is time for you to do your duty and contribute towards the survival of Acadia. It will not be so bad, you will see, and I will be so proud of you." The girl raised her head, it was Zahra, a younger Zahra with shorter hair. She was about sixteen years old. Her face was devoid of emotion, she nodded her head.

"I will make you proud grandfather."

Another image phased in, a dark-haired man. I only had a partial view of his profile. The man whose image just appeared held out his hand towards Zahra. She hesitated before placing her hand in his. His fingers closed around her hand. The images disappeared. I heard the screams of pain. Another image started to take shape, I gasped, it was Zahra, she was about to give birth. She threw her head back and screamed, her face contorted with pain. The images of two women appeared. I watched with a mixture of horror, sadness and joy as Zahra delivered twins. The strong cries of the infants filled the room. The two women who helped Zahra deliver her babies were holding them, soothing them.

"Well done, Zahra, you have given Acadia a son and a daughter. As is our custom, you may name them." Zahra lay back against the pillows exhausted, she stretched out her arms.

"Please let me hold them."

"You know the rules Zahra. You cannot become attached to them; they are not your children. You simply gave birth to them. They will receive the best of care from the family that raises them. Give them a name."

Zahra dropped her outstretched arms, silent tears streamed down her face. In a choked voice she said, *"Leah and Jacob."*

Heart wrenching sobs shook her body as she watched her babies being taken away. I was crying too, imagining the loss Zahra must be feeling. Her face started to fade; her image dissolved. Another image immediately followed; it was Zahra again standing in a bedroom looking at her reflection in a full-length mirror. She looked like she had when I saw her with Marcus. This was a current day image. She was wearing mustard-coloured silky PJs. She pressed her hands on her belly, a small smile curved her full lips. In a soft voice she said.

"I won't let them take you from me. Your father will help us, he is a good man. Strong and kind, he will help us – he must help us." A worried look crossed her face as her image faded. Dear God, Zahra was pregnant again. There was no clue about the father. Who is he?

I felt hands on my shoulders shaking me, I cried out and my eyes flew open. My body was drenched in sweat, the T-shirt and shorts I wore were stuck to me. My skin felt clammy and cold, even my hair was damp.

"Are you OK, was it a bad dream?" Kade was sitting beside me. The room was partly illuminated by the hallway light coming through the semi opened door. Kade turned on the bedside lamp. I brought my hand up to shield my eyes from the light whilst they adjusted.

"You are drenched! Are you ill?" He placed his hand on my damp forehead.

"No, I am fine." I shifted on the bed conscious that the dampness had seeped through the sheets to the mattress. Kade walked round to my side of the bed and helped me up.

"I am sorry, I have made a mess of the bed. I need a shower. I am sweating in places I have never sweated before."

"You were crying in your sleep thrashing around mumbling Zahra over and over."

"It was not a dream. Somehow, I connected to Zahra's thoughts." Tears rolled down my cheeks as everything that I had seen raced through my mind.

"Why don't you go and take a shower. Then we can talk. Don't worry about the bed, I'll strip it and put the sheets in the washing machine. Leave your clothes outside the bathroom door and I will put them in the machine too. I'll put some fresh clothes out for you in my room."

"Thanks." I went to the bathroom, stripped off my clothes and placed them outside the bathroom door for Kade. I washed my hair and took a quick shower. When I was done, I wrapped myself in a large towel and used a smaller towel to dry my hair. I looked at my image in the mirror. The colour of my eyes was particularly bright. I sent Soraya a cerebral message.

"Soraya, how can I connect to Zahra's mind? She's an Echoer; it shouldn't be possible."

"I don't know how it happened, Brissy, but you did connect to her mind, she was unaware of your presence. I am doing some analysis that might give us the answer to your question. I will update you in the morning."

I went into Kade's room. Kade was sitting in the armchair by the window. He stood up as I entered the room. It suddenly dawned on me that he was still wearing the same clothes he was wearing when I'd said good night to him.

I glanced at his alarm clock. It was 12:20 AM, I had been asleep for just over an hour. It felt a lot longer since I laid my head on the pillow.

"I thought it was later."

"You weren't asleep for long. Do you want a cup of tea?" I shook my head.

"No, thanks. Can I sleep with you?" Kade laughed softly. "You know what I mean, Kade."

"I do, and yes you can. I will be back in five minutes. I heard him go into the bathroom. I pulled on the fresh pair of shorts and T-shirt Kade left out for me. I brushed the tangles out of my slightly damp hair and secured it on top of my head. I got into his bed and lay facing his side of the bed. I walled in what I had seen, but some of the emotions were seeping through. I mustered sufficient control to be able to consider what I had seen.

Kade returned to the bedroom, I heard him undress, open his chest of drawers and close it again. He turned on the bedside lamp on his side of the bed then turned off the main lights and got into bed. He lay down and turned to face me. He was wearing PJ bottoms, but his chest was bare.

"Do you want to talk about what you saw?" I was silent for a moment, then responded in a quiet shaky voice.

"Yes." He took my right hand, brushed his lips against it and rested our intertwined fingers on his pillow. "I don't know how it happened, but I connected to Zahra's mind. I saw bits of her past and the present day." I took a deep breath trying to steady my shaking voice and working hard to keep the tears at bay. "I saw her when she was about sixteen, our grandfather gave her to some man. He said she had to do her duty for the survival of Acadia. The next images I saw were of Zahra giving birth to twins." My tears breached their barrier and were slipping slowly down my cheeks. Kade gently brushed them away with his thumb. "Kade - they took the babies away. They didn't even let her hold them." My voice broke, I paused, closing my eyes briefly. When I opened them again and looked at Kade, there was a sombre look on his face.

"One of the women who helped her deliver the babies said it was against the rules for Zahra to hold the babies, and that they were not her children. That she had simply given birth to them. They were to be given to a family to raise. Zahra named the twins Leah and Jacob. Her thoughts then returned to the present. She was standing in what I assume was her bedroom in PJs looking at herself in the mirror. She put her hands on her belly. She said she would not let them take her child. Then she said that the father would help her and the baby." Kade drew in a sharp breath and pulled me into his arms. I gave in to the tears and cried, he did not say a word just held me while I cried. My tears slowed and eventually stopped, I felt wrung out.

"I have to find a way to help her get away from him. How could he do that to her? He used her like an animal for breeding. What kind of a man would do that to a young girl? His own granddaughter!"

"It sounds pretty horrific; I am so sorry."

"Her life could just as easily have been my life, but for the fact that I was born first. Amon Gamal is not going to ruin her life any more than he has already. I now know why my grandmother sacrificed her life to smuggle my mother out of Egypt. If she hadn't, her life would have followed a similar pattern to Zahra's." Calmness began to seep through me. I had clarity.

"He is not taking Zahra's child, not again. I'm going to stop him. Whatever it takes." The decision was made, whatever it takes. I closed my eyes and welcomed sleep.

ಐಛ‍ಐ

17. HIJACKER

"What are your plans for today?" Kade asked as we stopped in front of my house. He pulled me into his arms. My arms circled his waist.

"Lots of studying. All this stuff is distracting me from what I really need to be focusing on. I don't want to fail my exams even if the idea of going to university is beginning to feel like a dream. I'll call Martha around 9:00 AM. I also have to attend my appointment with the optician at 12:00 PM.

"Don't doubt yourself, you can do this."

"Thanks." I smiled. He traced a finger along my nose. Our eyes connected. He held my gaze as he lowered his head to kiss me. My lids lowered as our lips touched. Our kiss was slow and deep. We drew apart slowly.

"I'll call you later. Call me if you want to talk. Try and get some rest too, I know you didn't sleep well last night."

"Thanks. Enjoy your run." He watched me unlock the door and enter. I gave him a final wave and shut the door quietly. It was early, there was no sign of life yet. I walked up the stairs quietly. My hand was on my bedroom door handle when Marcus came out of his room.

"Hello lose woman." His tone was teasing but there was a serious look in his eyes. He followed me into my room and shut the door.

"How are you doing?"

"I'm OK, thanks. What about you, Echoer?" Marcus shook his head.

"Not sure, still processing." I tried to broach the matter of Kade's status with him this morning. He gave me a similar response and changed the subject.

"I'm going to finish work early today. Why don't you meet me in town for lunch around 1:30 PM?"

"That would be nice. I'll come to your office. Don't forget to take a picture of the photo showing Zahra."

"I won't forget. I'm heading out early today so just a short run for me this morning. See you later."

"Later." I must ask him the question, but I don't know how. I need to know; I will have to ask when we meet this afternoon.

I stripped, took a quick shower, and dressed. Breakfast consisted of toast and coffee. I made a second mug of coffee and returned to my room with it. Sitting at my desk, I stared at the notice board attached to my desk. Various reminders were pinned to it together with a couple of group photos of me and the girls.

"Soraya, we need to talk."

"Good morning, Brissy." She appeared next to my desk. Dressed in her usual style of gown in a subtle grey.

"Morning. Have you figured out how I managed a cerebral connection with Zahra last night?"

"Not yet. I am still looking through the CC Link for clues."

"I feel like a lorry ran over me, backed up, and ran over me again." She observed me in silence.

"A lot has happened to you in just a few days. You should consider postponing the meeting with your grandfather."

"I can't do that. I may not get a chance to meet with him again any time soon. We have to go. Hoping Zahra will be at the meeting, I am dying to meet her."

"Meeting you sister will be a momentous occasion, I hope it goes well for you both."

"Thanks. What do you know about Martha?"

"The meeting with Martha did not go as I envisaged. I know you don't trust her. I have been digesting the discussion points. I agree with you that something is not right. My search of the CC Link now includes trying to find who the fifth Gene Bearer is, any mention of your parents and you. It's concerning that Zraykus got hold of a classified document naming your parents. The promptness of their attempted attack now makes sense. Kade is right. The level of risk Zraykus pose to you is higher than we thought. You need to be on your guard."

"Thanks Soraya. Martha mentioned that Guardians can only communicate with a Mutata's subconscious mind. You're different – why?"

"I am not entirely sure yet. I know that my bond to you is already unusually strong. The signs are that your path and therefore my path will differ from those that came before us. When the time is right, we will know what the divergence means. Follow your instincts on how much information you share with Martha. Despite the issues, you can still learn from her. You must still engage in your training."

"If I must work with her, I will. It may give me a chance to find out more than she is willing to tell me. I'm going to spend a couple of hours studying. I'll call her before 9: AM to set up another meeting."

"We will speak later."

"Wait! There's one more thing. How did I carve Zahra's birthmark into Kade's dining table?"

"I wanted to get more information before discussing it with you."

"More information, so you know something about it. What do you know?"

"I found information about a Mutata referred to as a wave shifter. My search is not complete yet, but it appears that the Mutata was channelling a huge amount of wave energy frequency, and weaponised it." A chill settled at the base of my spine.

"This Mutata was dangerous?"

"Yes. Please don't jump to conclusions, we need more information. Rest assured, it's a priority for me. Try not to worry about it."

"OK." She placed a hand on my shoulder, nodded, and was gone. Never going to ever get used to that!

I squeezed my eyes shut and took long deep breaths. My hands clenched into fists, my nails digging into my palms. Motionless, save for the rise and fall of my chest with each breath. You must park this Brissy, you have to! An image of a stormy sky popped into my head. I heard the clap of thunder as the clouds darkened. I will the storm away, I will the storm away. The words repeated in my mind until the storm diffused. The storm clouds drifted away; the sky lightened. My eyes slowly opened as if I was emerging from a deep sleep. I shook my head to clear the haze.

There was a knock at my door. I opened the door.

"Morning, Amada." I stood aside to let her in.

"Morning, honey. You look tired." Her sharp eyes scrutinised my face. "How are you doing?"

"I'm OK, thanks. The last few days have been difficult, but I am finding my feet. I'm OK."

"Unpicking all that surrounds your mother, and her death and dealing with it is going to be tough. I am very proud of you." She stepped close and drew me into a hug. I hugged her back. She had been such an unwavering presence for so many years. Giving unconditional love and support. Thank god for her. She released me slowly taking my hands and squeezing it.

"What do you have planned for today?"

"Studying this morning. Then my appointment with the optician followed by lunch in town with Marcus. Kade may join us. We may be a little late for dinner, we should be home by 8:00 PM.

"Good. I am making lamb chops. Why don't you invite Kade to join us?" My face beamed at her.

"Thanks, I will."

"Right, I'd better get dressed or I'll be late." She gave me a kiss on the cheek and left my room. She rapped on Grace's door. "Meet you in the kitchen in twenty minutes."

Reality was reinstated. Worry set in about how much work I needed to get through to secure my place at uni. Studying had been bumped far down my list of priorities. I'd convinced myself that I could get the grades needed, now I'm not so sure. There was a level of disassociation that was not there before. I needed to re-energise my investment in my goals.

I shut my door and returned to my desk. Right, two hours of focused study then I can spend a little time reading her diary. I hadn't started reading my mother's diary yet. Felt too emotionally battered to take much more. But I am in a different place now. A place of recognition and acceptance. What is to come will push me to the brink. I must push back and not lose myself.

My Law in Society final assignment paper was due in two weeks. I had done most of the legwork a couple of weeks back. It was time to pull it together. I picked up my notebook and planned the structure of my paper. As I jotted notes on the application of the rule of law to society, my mind drifted to the point made by Kade. Who are the judge and jury of the conduct of Gene Bearers? Focus Brissy. I gave myself a mental shake and brought my attention back to the task at hand. My focus was sustained for two hours. It was a good start, but more work was needed. I checked my phone; 9:15 AM, I was running a little late to call Martha. I made the call.

As expected, Martha agreed to meet with us. Her office at 6:00 PM. I sent Kade and Marcus a text confirming the meeting. Now for my prize, my mother's diary. I was home alone. I stood up and stretched reaching my arms high above my head. I wandered to my window and looked out and listened with my mind. The thoughts were of everyday life. People running late for work, organisation of the home and family. The content and discontent.

I took out my mother's diary and settled myself cross legged on my bed. I took in an audible deep breath and exhaled equally loudly before opening it. The handwriting was the same as the letter, neat, with elegant strokes.

October 20, 2002 - Rashidi has done it! He has isolated the wave energy frequency we need. His theory will work, I know it will. We just need time on our side. He has been working so hard, he is tired. I tried to get him to slow down but he won't. Our babies are due in May. Six months does not seem that long – we have so much to do.

November 11, 2020 – We tested it! The Shield Wave, that's what Rashidi is calling the new wave energy frequency we discovered. It works! We used it to shield a vase. The vase was not visible for two days. Our theory is that once refined and we can tap into enough of it, we can shield the girls and ourselves. It will give the ability to go unseen and, once absorbed in sufficient levels, it neutralises manipulation by other wave energy frequency.

December 15, 2020 – Every day we must memorise the developments and progress made. We cannot afford to have written records fall into the wrong hands. On a happy note, our girls are becoming quite active. It was wonderful to see the look on Rashidi's face when he felt them kick for the first time.

We have decided that each of the girls will have our mothers' first names and Rashidi's grandmother's name. I have known two mothers. The first to be born will be called Brissy Jayne and the other will be called Zahra Naomi. I still dream about her. Brave Zahra who risked all to give me a better life.

December 30, 2020 – Rashidi is unwell, he is losing weight and the tiredness is so much worse. The doctors are running tests. I am trying hard to contain my fear. A feeling of dread grows in me. He continues to work like a man who is almost out of time.

I closed the diary with trembling hands and sat still. I could feel tears welling up, I held them back. I am so sick of crying! I've cried more in the last few days than I have in the past six years. Enough with the bloody crying – no more! My phone rang.

I got up and picked it up from my desk. Kade.

"Hi, how was your run?"

"Good. You sound down, are you OK?"

"I am fine. I was reading my mother's diary, I guess I do feel a little sad. But I'm fine. Would you like to come to dinner tonight? I'm not sure how good the timing is bearing in mind we are seeing Martha. It was Amada's idea."

"I would love to come to dinner. Does that mean Amada does not hate me? I've been a little worried about what she thinks about you staying over last night." I laughed.

"Is big strong Kade afraid of my foster mother?"

"Let's just say I want to make a good impression. I don't have much experience of dealing with a girlfriend's mother. I know she is lovely from the couple of occasions I have met her. But the situation is different now."

"Relax. I know she is uncomfortable about me spending the night at your flat. But she didn't give me the third degree this morning. I know Amada, she will shelve her discomfort for now to focus on other priorities. Her priority is how I am coping with my mother's letter."

"How is the studying going?

"Not bad. I've put in a couple of hours. I'm going to put my mother's diary away and grab a mug of coffee and get back to it. Then I need to set off for my optician appointment. Meeting Marcus for lunch afterwards. What are you up to today?"

"Calls with three estate agents about the premises I need for my business. I also need to put the finishing touches to the business plan and complete my business loan application."

"Sounds like a busy day, I hope it all goes well. Me and Marcus will come to your flat around 5:00 PM. We need to be clear on what we want to discuss so we stay on point. If I start to look like I am going off the rails, you and Marcus need to rein me in. We have to get the information we need from her."

"Agreed. Are you going to tell Marcus about Zahra?"

"Yes. Hopefully, he can confirm he's not the father.

"Good luck. I will see you later masoyina."

"Masoyina?"

"It means my love in Hausa." My heart skipped a beat.

"That's very sweet." There was a little pause.

"Later."

"Bye." I couldn't stop smiling.

I returned my mother's diary to its hiding place and continued working on my paper. When I took my hands off the keyboard and leaned back in my chair, the paper was in reasonable shape. Three more points to incorporate, some editing and it would be done. A wave of tiredness washed over me. Need a nap before heading out for my appointment. I picked up my phone. I could get about an hour of shut eye and take a cab into town. I set an alarm and got into bed. Hopefully, there would be no dreams.

I woke with a start. I could hear someone moving around downstairs. Someone is in the house.

"Soraya, there is someone in the house." She appeared instantly.

"Get in the cupboard, try not to make any noise. I will go and investigate." I nodded and got up slowly, picking up my phone. Soraya disappeared. My heart was in my mouth as I crept to my desk taking care to avoid any creaking floorboards. I picked up my chair and made my way to the cupboard. I entered the cupboard and wedged the chair as tightly as I could under the door handle. I moved to the back of the cupboard and sat on the floor. Should I call the police? I might be heard speaking. I would wait until Soraya returned. I sent Kade and Marcus a text message making it clear that they should not call me. I turned my phone to silent mode. Where is Soraya? I listened intently; strange, I could not hear a mind in the house. I scanned the area. There was a man sitting in a van outside waiting for the intruder. Soraya appeared.

"He is placing listening devices and cameras around the house"

"I can't hear him Soraya, why can't I hear his thoughts?"

"His mind has been taken over. I will continue to watch him."

"I will call the police then Kade."

"OK, you should be fine to make the call without him hearing you." She vanished. I called the police. As quietly as I could, I explained the situation to them and told them about the man outside in the van. I asked if they could ask the officers dispatched not to use their sirens when they are close to my house. I was told the officers would use their judgment. I called Kade next.

"Brissy! are you OK? I'm almost at your house."

"I'm hiding in my bedroom cupboard. The police are on their way. The man is placing bugs downstairs, he will head upstairs soon. Listen, there's a van parked outside, there is another man sitting inside waiting for him."

"OK. Stay quiet and off the phone. I'm nearly with you." I heard footsteps on the stairs. I prayed he would go into Marcus' room first. My bedroom door open. I clamped my hand over my mouth. My heart was beating so fast it felt like it would burst out of my chest. The alarm on my phone went off. I jumped at the sound dropping my phone.

The handle of the cupboard door rattled. In the strongest voice I could muster I shouted.

"The police are on their way, get out of here while you can." No response. The door shuddered from an impact.

Fear was about to incapacitate me. Soraya appeared next to me making me jump.

"Brissy, if he gets in you have to fight. You must focus and stay in control. Deep breaths, that's it. Stand up; I will fight with you. But I can't fight unless you fight." I nodded taking deep breaths willing myself to calm down.

The door flew open, the chair was thrown at me knocking me off balance. I scrabbled to my feet. A young tall dark-haired man stood looking at me with vacant eyes.

"Hello Mutata, this is a surprise. The house was supposed to be empty, I thought you were shacked up with your boyfriend?" He smirked baring his teeth. "Let's get acquainted." He grabbed for me. I dodged his hands and flung the chair at him without touching it. He was knocked off balance falling out of the cupboard. I focused, visualising his body being dragged to the centre of my room and pinned to the floor. He started laughing.

"This just keeps getting better. You are telekinetic, what a rare find! Now I understand why Slater is so interested in you. The stakes have just been raised."

"Who are you? What do you want from me?" My voice regained its strength.

"Brissy!" I heard Kade yelling as he entered the house.

"Upstairs, Kade." He thundered up the stairs and entered my room. He took in the scene in a swift glance. He moved towards the man fists at the ready. His fists were bruised.

"It's OK, Kade, he can't move. What happened to your hands?" He reached for me and held me tight. I could feel the rapid beating of his heart against my cheek. My arms went around him. I closed my eyes briefly in relief.

"Are you OK?"

"Yes, I'm fine."

"I take it this is lover boy, where is the other one? I hear you are quite a popular girl." Kade moved to stand over him, his face twisted with fury.

"Kade, his mind has been hijacked, don't hurt him."

"Who is the cowardly bastard hiding behind this poor sod?"

"That's for me to know and for you to find out. You're like puppies floundering around. You don't have a clue what you are getting into. You've got some tough lessons ahead of you." His eyes moved to me. "Mutata, Slater wants you dead. Not sure why exactly, wasn't interested enough to ask. But now, I'm very interested. There are much better uses for you. You will not die at my hands or anyone else's until I've satisfied my curiosity." His eyes moved to Kade. "You on the other hand, I will happily take out for free." He gave another spine-chilling laugh. His eyes roamed around my room. His laughter ended abruptly. His eyes were fixed on my mother's photo on my desk. His gaze darted to me, then back to the photo. He looked at Kade.

"You're doing a piss poor job of keeping her safe." Kade smashed his fist into his face. Knocking him out cold.

"Kade! Why did you do that? I asked you not to hurt him." He stood up and looked at me. There was something in his eyes I'd never seen before. He turned his gaze back to the unconscious man on the floor.

"He was clearly not going to tell us anything else of use, and the police are here. You can't exactly say you pinned him down with your capabilities. Can you?" I had not noticed the sirens which were clearly audible now. So much for a quiet approach.

"What happened to your hand?"

"I knocked out the guy in the van." He took keys out of his pocket and waived them.

"Police! Brissy Jayne Yah, are you here?" Kade took my hand meeting my eyes.

"Keep it simple. Tell them everything that happened, as it happened save for the obvious." I nodded. "Showtime."

"Up here, officer." I called out.

ॐ∞ॐ

TTEO – the story continues, look out for Book 2 in the series.

Get new release updates, details of giveaways and more when you subscribe to my website –

www.renlaws.com

I hope you enjoyed my book. Please provide a review, it can be as long or as short as you like. Reviews help bring the book to the attention of other readers. You can leave a review on the platform you purchased the book on. Reviews can also be left on Goodreads.

THANK YOU
Ren Laws